The Warning

"Mr. Cavantalo," said Krongard, head of the political crime force. "Make absolutely no mistake about this. You won't be able to convince one *person what's going on. The few people with any actual knowledge are extremely good at their jobs and are just as patriotic as I am.*

"And one more thing. If you're saying to yourself, 'At least things can't get any worse,' don't listen. Because that little voice is dead wrong."

SCAPESCOPE

JOHN E. STITH

ACE SCIENCE FICTION BOOKS
NEW YORK

For Annette

SCAPESCOPE

An Ace Science Fiction Book / published by arrangement with
the author

PRINTING HISTORY
Ace Original / November 1984

ISBN: 0–441–75391–4

Ace Science Fiction Books are published by
The Berkley Publishing Group,
200 Madison Avenue, New York, New York 10016.
PRINTED IN THE UNITED STATES OF AMERICA

*"Prediction is very difficult,
especially about the future."*
— Neils Bohr

*"Everything that can be invented
has been invented."*
— Director of the
United States
Patent Office, 1899

chapter
ONE

Being summoned to Arthur Springer's office was probably a little like stepping into a dark elevator shaft. Right away I got a bad feeling, and even though I couldn't see what was coming, there were strong indications that the situation would worsen. Arthur never called in any of his subordinates when good news was on the way.

What usually annoyed me about Arthur was that he was a GS-68 while I was just a GS-56. Today I would have been grateful to be merely annoyed, because something much worse was disturbing me.

It might all be starting today. I was afraid that Sal might have been right when she told me I'd be fired soon. And that wasn't the worst of it.

The narrow one-way slidewalk had almost carried me past Arthur's office before I realized how far I'd come. A quick step landed me in Arthur's beige-and-tan outer office. His secretary, Rob Tannoy, greeted me.

"Any idea how long it's going to be this time?" I asked him, even though I already had a fair guess.

"Maybe five minutes." Rob returned to his work. I would have asked him what it was all about, but Arthur wouldn't have told him. Arthur loved surprises, as long as he wasn't the last to know.

I had to admire Rob. No matter how unbearable Arthur was, Rob was always in good humor. Rob was a thin fellow, partway through his twenties and somewhere in his GS-30s. His straight blond hair and his shorts and T-shirt made him look as though he should still be in school. He was one of those people whose rating changed about as fast as his height, but he never seemed to let Arthur dampen his spirits.

Perhaps to counteract Arthur's negativity, Rob had started a graffiti collection and usually had one or two samples on his wall screen. Today's entrées were "Tele-kinesis is a moving experience," and "I'd give my right arm to be a cyborg." After I thought about it, I wondered if maybe they were more for the benefit of Arthur's visitors. Surely quite a few of them could use a little cheering up.

I sat down on a water-cushioned chair. Waiting was becoming one of my least favorite activities. It gave my mind time to wander. And to wonder when things were going to start heading downhill. At least scapescope said that my GS rating wouldn't start to drop for several more days.

After that, anything could happen.

It annoyed me enough that Arthur routinely made people with appointments wait. What angered me more was to have to wait after being called to his office. Still, my mood would have been better if that were the worst of Arthur's habits.

I might not have been feeling so frustrated if it hadn't been for the crank calls all night long. Some joker had found out how to override the normal filters for non-emergency calls and had kept me awake and highly irritated. Take the constant fear of Sal's predictions, add having to endure Arthur's habits while half asleep, and the sum far exceeded my irritation quotient.

Needlessly I checked my wristcomp for other appointments. It confirmed what I already knew: nothing on the immediate horizon.

Rob's voice brought me back to the problem at hand. "Hey, Mike. His Highness will see you now."

I looked up in time to catch his wink. "Thanks." I set my wristcomp to busy just in case I got any calls.

After a halfhearted attempt to push my lips closer to a mild grin, I slid aside the door to the inner office. I was tempted to call out, "Are you decent?" but neither my mood nor Arthur's sense of humor was up to it.

"Hello, Arthur." It was "Arthur," never "Art." I wouldn't call him "Mr. Springer," but I did make the smaller concession. As usual he put on his brief show of being incredibly industrious, so I looked around the office rather than look at the thinning spot in the unwashed brown hair on top of his head. I felt almost as comfortable as a patient being examined by an absentminded veterinarian. High on one wall an electrostatic air cleaner hummed almost imperceptibly, trying to eliminate the stale odor.

His office barely held three straight-backed visitors' chairs in addition to Arthur's chair and desk. His rating entitled him to fifty percent more space than I had, and the extra seats took most of it. The walls were so sparsely decorated, I soon swiveled my gaze back to Arthur.

His ironic appearance made me suppress a grimace. The navy-blue T-shirt couldn't hide his ninety-kilo bulk. His weight not only placed him a couple of standard deviations above the norm; it made him look more like

Santa Claus than any other man I knew. Arthur was short: short-tempered, shortsighted, and he had a short attention span.

I was thinking about Sal when Arthur finally looked up.

"Hello, Mike." Never "Michael," never "Mr. Cavantalo."

I wasn't going to ask why he'd called me. He would tell me when he wanted to. And it was impossible to change his timetable.

With clipped, economical motions he placed a second screen on his desk and positioned it for me to see. Arthur had a genuine time-and-motion obsession. I liked to think of it as motion sickness.

He looked at me for the first time. "I have high standards for the reports that come out of this department." He paused. "This one doesn't come close." Arthur's brown eyes blinked as he talked, another sure sign of trouble.

He must have been referring to the thirty-day photonic engineering forecast. It was the only report that I had turned in during the last few days.

"Arthur, I busted my budget preparing that forecast. What don't you like about it?"

"Just the fact that it is sloppy, poorly worded, and it seems that you didn't even find time to proofread it."

"I think there must be some mistake."

In answer he spoke a command to his console. The header and the first few lines of my report appeared on the screen. He gave it another command and the text scrolled to page three.

"Have a look at the second paragraph," he said, and unnecessarily started reading it aloud for me. "I rrrecommend that efforrrts be moved frrrom parrrallel prrrocessorrrs to—"

His sarcastic rolling *r*'s didn't improve my mood at all. "I think I can explain—"

"Oh, I do hope so." Arthur leaned back in his chair and rested his head on the wall. If he had been a cat, he would have played with his food.

"Somehow you've got my first draft. The voice recognition unit on my office terminal was having problems, and it hadn't been fixed then. My first drafts are very rough. What I *don't* understand is how you got that text instead of my final version."

"Even if I believed this is only a draft, why do you imply that this was *my* mistake?"

"Oh, no, I didn't mean to say that *you've* made a—Wait a minute. What do you mean 'even if you believed me'?" I was thoroughly puzzled. Why was he making such an issue of the mix-up?

"I mean the whole story sounds fabricated to me. Look, Mike. If you're too busy or too tired or whatever to finish your work, just say so."

Sometimes there was only a fine line between having deep-seated convictions and being opinionated. Occasionally it seemed as simple as whether or not a person agreed with my views, but objectively I knew there was more to it. Actually it mattered whether or not the person really listened to opposing viewpoints, and if he or she realized that a given individual perceived a situation in terms of personal values.

Arthur came nowhere near that fine line.

"Arthur, I don't know how this version got transmitted, but it's a genuine mistake. I'm conscientious about my work. You surely know that by now. I'll get back to my office and find out what happened. You'll have the right draft in an hour or two."

"I need it yesterday." Standard response number four.

A visit with Arthur was a little like taking a moon walk. He lived in a high-contrast world in which everything was black or white, clearly defined or unimportant. The way I saw it, he didn't have enough gray matter to evaluate subtle shades of gray.

"I'll get it to you as soon as I can, all right?"

"I'm going to be watching you closely, Mike. You'd better watch your step." Arthur pursed his lips, popping them and following up with a sigh.

I still didn't understand why he was so upset, but somehow the time didn't seem right to try to find out.

"I'll get it to you soon."

Arthur pursed his lips again but didn't reply, so I took that as a cue to leave.

On my way out I gave a mock salute to Rob. His wry smile seemed to say, "Have a good day in spite of him, if you can."

It must have been a quiet day, because the slidewalk was motionless when I stepped onto it. As it lurched gently forward, I canceled the hold on my calls. No one had tried to reach me during my audience with King Arthur.

This was one of the many times that I regretted the transfer that had brought me into Arthur's department late last year. Prior to the move, a couple of people had told me, "He's a really nice guy once you get to know him." That turned out to mean, as is sometimes the case, that he's inconsiderate and rude to everyone except the few people whom he likes well or needs. And it hadn't helped matters when he made the pass at Sal. But even allowing for his overbearing manner, this most recent development was excessive.

Why the overreaction, though? And how could he have received the wrong draft? My normal practice was to purge all early drafts as soon as the final looked good and I had copies.

Why is nothing ever easy? Surely there must be an easier way to earn (or at least get) a living. I was one of the eight out of every ten adult workers who were employed by Brother Sammy. It seemed like things must have been a little easier back when he was simply a more distant uncle. Good old B.S.

One of the nice things, however, about the number of civil service jobs was that, with as many jobs as there were, quite a few of them were bound to be interesting.

Despite Arthur's fits, my job wasn't a bad one. I was a photonics engineer/futurist. Which simply meant that I used my photonics education in conjunction with whatever scapescope could show of the future. Then I prepared reports that affected the direction in which current photonic research traveled.

Unfortunately scapescope was not confined to the sciences.

A fast circular elevator dropped me down to my level. The door opened onto a beige-and-brown corridor much wider and busier than Arthur's. I took the slide-walk to my office. The door slid shut behind me and I leaned on it for several minutes, rubbing my eyes. I left my T-shirt on despite the warmth in the enclosed two-meter-square space. My height wasn't above average, but the room felt small.

Still puzzled about what had happened to my report, I folded my desk down from the wall and told my office phone to start accepting calls again. I almost slid out my keyboard, but instead I found myself turning on my scapescope.

Not paying much attention, I set it for about a week uptime. For a few minutes I simply watched the rows of text, some of them fuzzy, some of them vividly clear.

Scapescope was an overwhelming tool. Celeste Newbury and André Kalmez had made the breakthrough less than twenty years ago, in the late 2130s. They had been investigating fields generated by some family of subatomic particles when serendipity stumbled in.

Scapescope had revolutionized too many specialties to count. And it did far more than that.

It let the human race see its future.

To be accurate, it let the human race see the *futures*. Anything might or might not happen, and every event had a probability associated with it.

What I mean is, it might be a toss-up as to whether or not a flipped coin would land tails up, but it was very likely that the coin would fall. Via scapescope events to come were visible. The trouble was that *all* events to come were there, superimposed.

The net result was that groups of improbable outcomes obscured one another, while foregone conclusions were startlingly clear. Events with probabilities between the two extremes were often visible. Subject to noise in the Newbury–Kalmez field, we could see quite a way uptime. When the noise was low, probable events could be seen as far uptime as six months.

What was bothering me right then was the cliché about no news being good news. I would rather have had no news than the news it provided about me.

I flicked off scapescope and uneagerly turned my thoughts back to the monthly report. A few minutes at the terminal were enough to show that my first draft had found its way into the file reserved for the final report. Not only that; there weren't any other drafts on file.

My only recourse was to revise the text. The work went relatively fast since the contents were still fresh in my memory and the initial text was still there. The voice recognition module was working better now. Occasionally the terminal would say, "Huh?" if I didn't pronounce a word clearly enough, but that was normal.

As I worked, my subconscious kept tugging me back to Arthur. He had always been the type of guy whose GS level was consistently exceeded by his BS level, but he had been intolerant today, even on his scale. I examined each of the items in the report as I reconstructed it, to see if any of them might have touched a nerve with Arthur.

Everything seemed fairly routine. Scapescope showed that the Anderson very-high-density optical character reader project would show significant results in less than six weeks. I had recommended that funding be continued. Jorgenston wouldn't be so happy. Scapescope indicated that his catalytic energy conversion efforts would be unsuccessful for as far as we could see uptime. Those funds could be transferred to other projects with better chances for success. At least we didn't have to funnel funds down a dead end like we used to.

I finished the text and, just to be sure, copied it into two other files and protected each of them with a unique password. Then I sent a copy to Arthur's office.

Once again drawn to the scapescope, I turned it on, set it for a month uptime, and peered at the characters displayed. Newbury and Kalmez had coined the term "scapescope," evidently while thinking about seeing future landscapes displayed on a scope. That must have been before they realized how little value it would have for that purpose.

The only views of the future that were of any use were not actual pictures. They were simple alphanumeric character strings. With the right equipment, physical actions could be seen for a few seconds uptime, but after that there were far too many variables. John Doe might scratch his nose at 1202:43, or maybe 1203:22. To solve the problem, the bright boys and girls had come up with the Current Events Display.

The CED was a daily summary of every significant event that could be listed by using a twenty-four-hour time frame. By knowing what time of day a particular summary was scheduled (for instance, deaths were scheduled for 0810:00), one could search for whatever information was available. Clear lines denoted the most probable happenings. Every day a huge display was updated for everyone downtime to see.

Inadvertently I had called up the marriages section. I switched it off hastily. That was stupid. I already knew what wouldn't be there, even if Sal and I had been that serious before she got the news.

I also knew that I had to get out of the office for a while. My last act was to call Arthur to make sure he had gotten the correct report this time. Rob answered the phone and scanned the report before saying goodbye. I folded up my desk and left.

Quite a few people were already at the GS-50 through -65 cafeteria when I arrived. I picked up a few things at an idle dispenser. As I looked for a chair Seldon Lanyard's wave caught my eye, so I joined him. He was as thin as ever, but he was short enough to make his proportions reasonable.

"Hey, Mike. How are you doing?" Seldon worked in weather engineering. His office handled most of the southern Maryland district. He was a good friend, but I hadn't seen very much of him for several months. Sal had taken up most of my free time, and since she left I had been hibernating.

"Oh, getting by."

"I haven't seen you or Sal for way too long. What have you been up to?"

I couldn't lie to Seldon, but the problems weren't something I felt like discussing. "Ah, there's been a snag. She moved out. Could we talk about it some other time?"

"Sure. I'm awfully sorry. Do you want to talk at all?" Seldon would never push. He had broken out of his tense constant-pressure period. A few years ago he had put in so much time at work that his wife almost expected to get a ransom note.

"How's the weather lately?" I said with brilliant originality.

"Business as usual. How's soothsaying?"

"Not very soothing sometimes."

"What now?"

"That's 'who now.' Arthur Springer. He's on the rampage because of a mix-up on one of my reports. And I can't find out why it's such a big deal. He's got his beltline up to his eyebrows, so he interprets almost anything I say as criticism."

"I thought he was like that all the time."

"Maybe a little, but this seems worse than ever." And maybe there was more to it than that.

"Well, let me know if you'd like to work some frustrations out on the courts." Seldon didn't look athletic, wearing his conservative trousers and slouching a bit at the table. He was almost ten years older than I, his hair prematurely graying, but he was probably in better shape. I liked to stay fit, but not when it seemed like work.

"Right. And thanks, Seldon." He was a good listener with sharp instincts. I probably should have gone, but at the moment I just wanted more time to puzzle out the whole situation with Arthur.

I ate the rest of my meal without saying much more. Seldon evidently sensed my need for quiet.

"Thanks for the company. I'll try to be more talkative next time." I rose to leave.

"Anytime. Let me know if you want to talk."

"Thanks. Oh, say hi to Connie." I left Seldon in the cafeteria and went back to my apartment several floors up.

At home the reflections on the walls greeted me. The mirrors in the room were my attempt to conceal the fact that my apartment was only four meters square. My reflected alter ego looked tired. I pushed some blond hairs back into place, uncovering a few worry lines.

Emotionally and physically exhausted, I settled into the hideaway bed, flipped on the news, and widened the story-selection criteria. There were a few routine items. Petitions for a steeper population diminishment rate. Scapescope had revealed enough information to justify arresting a small group foolish enough to be planning a murder. Congress increased the maximum GS level to eighty-one—between longevity increases and inflation, the maximum seemed to climb at least one level every five years. A plaintiff in a big lawsuit was unlucky enough to lose, so he was having to pay the defendant the sum he had sued the other for.

One story caught my attention. Celeste Newbury was missing. Her scapescope brainchild had made disappearances like that predictable and therefore rare, but I guessed that a recluse could drop out of sight more easily than could a ten-to-fiver.

I wished I hadn't turned on the news. That last item reminded me of scapescope—the very last thing I wanted to think about. Make that almost the very last.

Sal was the very last.

Sal Vienta and scapescope. What a pair.

Like a bird swooping toward a light in the darkness and then slamming into a window, I felt my thoughts drawn to the pair, only to run into a scapescope screen.

It was less than a week since Sal had moved out—because of something she saw on her law-enforcement scapescope. Before too much longer I was going to be fired. After that, my name would be found on a list of known political criminals.

And that particular line was absolutely clear.

chapter
TWO

It was less than a week since I had first found out that something was seriously wrong. Sal and I had planned to go to a concert that night, but she returned from work almost two hours later than usual. She was unusually quiet, so I tried to find out what the trouble was.

In a bigger apartment she might have just tried to hide for a while. In our four-by-four there wasn't anyplace to hide. After several attempts to draw her into conversation, I sensed that I might be making her feel as if she shouldn't have come home at all, so I shut up. We had lived together for only a couple of months, and I probably didn't know all her moods.

Sal was an unusual combination; she possessed strong career goals, but she could usually leave her work behind when she came home. She was normally an imperturbable, calm woman who took upsets in stride, so whatever it was had to be significant and unpleasant. The silence lasted long enough to make me feel as uncomfortable as she looked. At first she seemed worried, almost scared. Then fear apparently gave way to anger during the next few minutes.

She made several false starts, as though she wanted to talk, but didn't know how to start or what to say. Finally she began to explain.

"It's still all so hard to believe. I was late because I checked it and double-checked it until I couldn't see straight." She stopped for breath, her eyes focused on her hands shaking slightly in her lap.

"Don't stop now," I said.

Sal took another deep breath. "I don't know what you're planning, but I've got to get out, before you actually do anything." She was almost hyperventilating by then.

"Planning? What do you mean, 'planning'?"

"Oh, come on, Mike. You run a scapescope yourself. You know as well as I do, it's just not possible to conceal activity like that."

"Activity like what? What the hell's going on? Just tell me what you're talking about."

"Don't pretend you don't know. I saw it on my scapescope. You're on the political criminal list—less than two months uptime. I still can't believe it." She pushed her dusty-blond bangs aside so she could dry her eyes.

I was momentarily speechless. Her story was 100 percent surprise to me. But Sal was certainly in a position to know. She had a dual-skill job like mine, except that her combination was futuristics and law enforcement.

"Sal, just slow down and relax. There's got to be a mistake here, or several. I've got absolutely no intention of turning subversive. Hey, look at me. This is good old Michael Cavantalo. I'm as honest as this apartment is small." She didn't look convinced in the slightest. I guessed that I didn't sound very convincing since it was hard to take the situation seriously.

"Mike, a person can get on the homicide list in a lot of ways, quite a few of which don't require premeditation. But not the political list. You don't just go wacko and start a subversive group or something. Those things take time."

"So, maybe that's true. But if my name is on that—"

"It's there all right."

Once again I couldn't find anything to say, so I got up and paced while I tried to piece it together. Nothing made any sense.

"You're sure it's me—I mean it's my ID number and everything—not some other Mike Cavantalo?"

"Mike, listen to me. I checked it all the way down. That's your name." Her jade-green eyes were misty, but still she wasn't crying.

It was impossible. I had no dangerous visions of toppling an overgrown government or assassinating the President. I didn't even sign petitions. I still couldn't take it seriously.

Yet Sal was sure. And I knew her. She was thorough and competent, so what did that leave? Sal was totally honest—that was part of what initially attracted me.

"Okay. I'll believe you. You say my name is on the list, so I'll accept that. But it must be a clerical error or some other mistake. I've never had any aspirations to become a criminal."

Then I realized that I was talking to her back. So much for backtalk, I thought crazily.

"Hey, are you listening to me?" I peered over her shoulder so I could see what she was doing. She was packing.

"Yes, I heard you. But I know they don't make clerical mistakes like this one. And don't you think that if it was a simple mistake that sometime in the next few weeks they'll take care of it? Face it, Mike. It's going to happen."

"What are you doing?" I asked, knowing exactly what she was doing, but not why.

"I've got to leave. If we're together when it happens, I'll be up to my eyebrows in trouble. And I can say fare-well to my career."

I understood then. Living with a criminal would cer-tainly smother an otherwise promising law-enforcement career. But knowing why didn't give me any comeback, snappy or otherwise, that would make her want to come back.

I also knew then that nothing I could do or say would make the slightest difference. Sal was perhaps the most stubborn person I knew. She was not only obstinate, she was proud of it, calling it self-confidence. I simply sat and watched, numb.

My attention began to tighten, and for no reason I began to focus on details. I found myself staring at her fingernails. They were rainbows lately, since she changed her drugdye color every week. Gradually I lost track of what was happening in the room.

Much later I found that I was again aware of the surroundings. It was so quiet I could hear my pores breathe.

I hadn't seen her since.

I had gone down to work as soon as I could, to see it for myself, but Sal had been right, of course. There was no way to find out how my name got on the list, but there it was. I'd believed her, but there's no substitute for firsthand observation. I spun in circles trying to find out why, but I couldn't figure out where to start.

The only thing I could think to do was probably

futile, but I felt compelled to do *something*. I found a brass frog in a shop and sent it to Sal, along with a note that said, "Before I met you, I felt like a frog. There were times with you when I felt like a prince. I'm NOT going to be on that list."

It wasn't until later that I recalled the old saying about women having to kiss a few frogs before finding a prince. By then it was too late to get it back.

I lost a lot of sleep, spending long hours thinking about Sal, and immersing myself in self-analysis. One by one I tried to put each of my values under intensive examination, attempting to find some tiny clue that might explain why I seemed destined to a fate worse than debt.

Nothing. I didn't think that I was necessarily a model citizen, but I wasn't all that unhappy with the status quo. Sure, I got irritated once in a while, but the mood always passed.

Probably everyone was unhappy about the lack of space, but conditions would have been a good deal worse if it hadn't been for the Suitcase Wars. Before then, the planet had been known as Smother Earth.

No matter how hard I tried, I just could not visualize myself on the criminal list.

I kept plowing through my regular activities, finding it hard to concentrate. A few days passed before the first break in my routine.

I had settled in for the evening when a chirp from my mailbox signaled an incoming message. My sister, Patricia, had finally written again. It was good to hear from her, but I felt so lethargic that I threw the note onto the wall screen rather than prop myself up and use the desk viewer.

It had been quite a while since I'd seen Pat, but we were probably as close as brother and sister were likely to be. Our parents never did say what qualifications they had possessed to justify two offspring, but we had found ourselves unusual enough to frequently feel left out of activities. For reasons that weren't always understandable, each of us preferred the company of the other, or of the few other pairs of siblings that we knew. We both became more independent as we grew older, but the interdependence had felt comfortable at the time.

The letter didn't say much, but I knew it was from her. She used the first-letter code we had adopted to insure that our communications were not forged. Pat was healthy and happy, but she still didn't say where she was or what she was doing.

All of our recent contacts were via a blind-drop system that even Brother Sammy couldn't trace. In spite of, or maybe because of, the massive population, quite a few people were privacy nuts. I respected Pat's privacy partly because I had no choice.

The letter itself was typical, but I was puzzled by her closing. Even after I had the dictionary look up "hyperopic," I didn't understand her reference to a rare eye defect.

I switched the screen back to a mirror state and noticed that my reflection wore a slight grin. It did feel good to hear from Pat again, even just to know that she was happy doing whatever she did. With that realization came another.

I wasn't going to let the situation overcome me. No one told Michael Cavantalo that his world was going to hell and he was helpless to do anything about it. But I'd have to do it all myself. There wasn't anyone who would be able to tell me to take two aspirins and call back in the morning.

Suddenly the small apartment felt even more confining. Maybe a walk would clear my head and help me figure things out. I changed clothes, left the apartment, and started down to the indoor park on the fortieth floor—the outdoor parks were always packed.

The annunciator near the elevators told me which one was most likely to get to my level first, and it was right. What it didn't tell me was that the elevator contained a bored youth passing out Negative Population Growth leaflets. I studiously ignored him after stuffing one into my pocket.

When I got to the park, I stored my sandals in a locker and wandered in. The breeze and the feeling of spaciousness were refreshing. Parks were about the only places where the air moved fast enough to be called wind. Grass tickled the soles of my feet. The chamber housing the park was immense. It was large and acoustically designed to eliminate the normally inescapable echoes.

Maybe I never totally let go in the park. I enjoyed the illusions, but part of me was always examining the surroundings, trying to tell which portions were real and which were holo projections or mirrors. The blending was skillfully done.

It was a good time to be there. Very few other people roamed the park. Behind me a couple and their daughter laughed loudly enough for me to hear. Ahead was an enforcer in his blue T-shirt and shorts, apparently off duty.

For the first hour or so I was fairly oblivious to time and my worries about Arthur's reactions. The grass, the trees and shrubs, and the lake managed to merge into a relaxing mass of greens and blues. I could feel the back of my neck relax finally, and I wondered what I would have looked like in Arthur's office if I had a ruff of hair—probably like an angry dog with the fur standing up on the back of its neck.

Even the park couldn't completely subdue my fears, though. All it took was a glimpse of a woman whose hair glimmered like Sal's to drop me back into my rut. Against my will, a vaguely similar scene sprang back to life.

The week Sal and I had met, we spent almost half of our time in a park. The time had cost me a day's pay, but that thought hadn't even occurred to me. We talked forever. A curious mixture of similarities and differences reinforced feelings of commonality and curiosity. We both felt an urgency to be proficient at our jobs and rarely made close friends who didn't share or at least understand the same urge.

Sal had a protective layer of isolation that at once attracted and repelled me. I felt honored to be allowed to get close to her in a way that others hadn't, and I envied her ability to avoid letting the myriad of day-to-day annoyances depress her. It was quite a while before I started wondering if I were really on the inside of her shell. If I was on the inside, I had gotten there via osmosis—I don't think the shell ever cracked for anyone.

After a couple of hours in the park I was feeling even worse than when I had gone in. I had managed to grab hold and stop the self-analysis briefly when I made a disconcerting observation.

After all that time of wandering around the park, I was still in sight of an enforcer.

He was nearly fifty meters away, but he looked very much like the one who had been near me earlier. You're never alone with paranoia. Out of curiosity I decided to walk awhile longer. To make it interesting I made it a random walk, using the digits in my identification number to determine the direction to take when choices were available.

I was angry by the time the first five numbers had gone, (even for left, odd for right). When I got to the twelfth, I was furious.

The enforcer was still there, a discreet fifty meters away.

One more realization came to me then. Sal knew I was going to be on the political criminal list. I knew about it. Surely other law enforcement officials knew about it too. Somehow the probability of being watched by the government gave a whole new meaning to the phrase "Brother Sammy wants *you*."

chapter
THREE

The surveillance thoroughly annoyed me, but what bothered me most was, Why didn't they just use electronic or photonic devices? Why do it in person? Or were they using both?

The answer would have to wait. The only possibility that came to mind was that they merely wanted to antagonize me. Anything was possible, but I wasn't able to persuade myself that enforcers would waste their time for such a weak reason.

They could very easily be using bugs in addition to the enforcer following me. In fact, they probably were. My normal activities shouldn't arouse their interest, but to be safe I decided that I should watch my step. Discouraged, I started back to my apartment to try to get some sleep. It was amazing how often I had been using the concept of "they."

On the way up to my level I leaned on the elevator wall. The elevator had risen past half of the thirty levels on the way when abruptly a high-pitched whine sounded, and the elevator stopped. Silence followed.

I waited a moment for it to start up again. When it didn't, I finally pressed the emergency communications button. No response. I pressed it several more times.

My wristcomp was no help either. It was hard to believe, but I couldn't reach anyone from inside the elevator. I was certain that I had made calls from elevators before, but right then nothing was happening.

I stood for twenty minutes, figuring that at any moment someone in a distant control room would look up at a status panel and see a red light. My legs grew so tired from standing, I finally sat down. After that, I lay down on the floor.

I never did go to sleep, partly because of my anger, partly because of the pain in my legs. It was nearly impossible to get comfortable in a circular one-meter-diameter elevator. When the elevator came back to life almost twelve hours later, I was already late for work. I called in a complaint on my way to the office, but the technician didn't sound as if he took me seriously. My frustration level was riding dangerously high, and I hadn't even started work yet.

I was achingly tired by the time I sat in my chair. The first message to come up after I unfolded my office and logged on was from Arthur. He wanted an evaluation of the progress on the Kipple lens project. And naturally he wanted it "yesterday." I decided that today I would interpret "yesterday" to mean "by noon" and started on it.

The work went reasonably fast. Kipple submitted progress reports frequently, and his were more understandable than those of his peers. The project itself was practical but not very interesting. Its end result was a subminiature lens for fiber cable repeaters. A better lens certainly would be useful and cut costs, but it wasn't as exciting as any of the glamour projects.

By 1130 I finished the evaluation and, bearing in mind the last fiasco, saved several copies with different identification names and passwords. When I was finished, I sent a copy to Arthur's office and flagged it as a priority message.

Too tense to eat lunch, I tried to relax during the half hour. By the end of lunch break it was all I could do to keep my eyes open. The lack of sleep was catching up with me.

I tried to restart my metabolism and began efforts in a new direction, hoping that Arthur the Pyromaniac wouldn't light any fires that afternoon. The occurrence of my name on the criminal list could only be a mistake. I had to find out the steps that led there.

The menu defaults came up on the scapescope screen. I pronounced the words "law enforcement," and a second menu came up. Selecting the words "criminal activities" should have started me the way I wanted to go.

All I received for my trouble was the message, "Update in progress—please try later."

That was unusual. Normally there were two or three more submenus, followed by the requested lists. I didn't recognize the error message, but even if it were accurate, I thought I should have been able to go all the way through the menu.

Fortunately the cross-indexing was so thorough that I could get to some of the same data by starting at PHOTONICS CURRENT TOOLS, tracing through SURVEILLANCE TECHNIQUES and eventually winding up at PENDING ACTIONS. I found my name on the list labeled CONFIRMED CRIMINALS—POLITICAL.

The line of text was still perfectly legible.

I held the forward button down while I watched the day of the year at the top of the screen count upward toward two hundred. Gradually the line with my name on it grew fuzzier, along with the rest of the names on the page. Apparently there would be no reprieve during the predictable future. I started scanning backward to see when my name first appeared on the list.

It was less than two weeks uptime, but it was vague and indistinct. Six weeks uptime it was as clear as any other entry on the list. So the exact date that I would make it onto the list was not definite, but I'd be on it within six weeks for sure.

With the scapescope set for one day uptime, I started the laborious process of checking every name to see if I knew anyone already on the list. The computer could have scanned the list and flagged any match with my phone list, but I knew quite a few people I didn't call regularly or at all.

Nothing turned up. I must have been associating with a fairly tame group of people.

Remembering the codes by each name, I recalled the display and looked at mine. G-10. It took a few minutes to find the list of designations. I shouldn't have bothered; G-10 was the catchall category. It was nice to know that I wouldn't definitely go out and murder a politician, but I really didn't feel well informed.

On impulse I scanned pending deaths and executions. At least my name wasn't on that list—yet.

I was entering another request when the door chirped. I slid it open and was surprised to see Harlan Dalbieto standing on the narrow strip adjacent to the slidewalk, ready for his shift.

"Hi. Is it that late already?" I asked, glancing at my wristcomp. I was still tired, but sitting had been better than being folded into an elevator.

"You workaholics are all alike. How about making some room for me? All this wonderful stuff will be here tomorrow too.'' The beard he scratched was so full that it almost covered his grin.

My office was now Harlan's office. With space at such a premium, most offices and all labs were used for three or four shifts. For now, I had days, Harlan had swings, and Deb Hillary had mids. Next year I was due for swings.

"Okay, okay." I switched off the scapescope. Harlan was pleasant enough, but we never seemed to have much to discuss, because our interests were so different. I didn't think he would know how to read if the job didn't require it. He had never mentioned reading a novel.

I said good-bye and stepped onto the hall slidewalk. It carried me fifty meters while I tried to decide what to do next. I was tired, but very hungry.

There wasn't anyone I knew in the cafeteria. After the meal I thought briefly about going back to my apartment and just going to bed, but sleeping would probably lead to dreams of Sal, and I needed a break to take my mind off my troubles for a while.

It took me several long agitated moments before I was willing to get back on an elevator, but finally I rode the elevator up to the seventy-fifth level and took the slidewalks for about ten minutes before arriving at the main neighborhood game room.

The several sections devoted to team games were in the front. I elbowed through, trying to decide what to play, and someone called my name. I looked past a few heads and saw Seldon with a holopolo stick in his hand.

"How about a game?" he asked.

That sounded good. Maybe I had been hoping to find him there. I nodded and went to pick out a stick while he reset the table. He broke, but nothing went in.

I saw a position I liked and moved around the table. "What's the action set to?"

"Five," he replied.

Which meant that I needed a medium–light stroke. I slid the cue stick toward the ball and watched the cue ball image take off, hitting the three ball with a glancing blow. The three ball vanished into the corner pocket and the score display changed. I watched as the cue ball rolled to a stop much sooner than I had expected.

"Nice guy. You must have the friction set up to eight or nine," I complained.

"A person has to have a little challenge." Seldon may have needed more of a challenge than I did. His left eye was augmented, a synthetic replacement. The inhumanities that had resulted from the early organ banks put extreme pressure on replacement research, and the substitutes worked better than the originals. The only problem now was that the government had to discourage deliberate self-disfigurement by people who wanted improved eyesight or hearing or whatever. The most common deterrent was to limit those cases to repair, if possible, or just let them do without.

I missed the next shot. As Seldon prepared to shoot I almost wished he had never shown me that antique table. Right then I felt like really pounding something. That old table—they had called it pool then, not polo—with its solid balls would have been more satisfying.

The holopolo table used the same rules, but somehow a computer-controlled holographic simulation didn't have the same feel. All the balls were projections shuttled around the table by a program that took into account the speed, angle, and English you put on the cue ball when your stick struck its projection.

The cue ball image accelerated fast enough to avoid the stick, but I would have been happier if the stick met the resistance caused by actually whacking the thing.

"You feeling any better yet?" Seldon asked.

I was about to reply when I caught sight of an enforcer uniform. "Hard to say. I've had more time to adjust, but it's still quite a shock."

He lined up another shot. With mathematical precision that forever eliminated all excuses about bad cushions, dirty surfaces, dented balls, and off-level tables, the holopolo computer shuttled the images around the table with faultless regularity.

Once in a while I liked to set the friction to zero and the action to ten. If the cue ball stayed out of the pockets, I could sink all the balls with one shot. And it could take as little as thirty seconds. On days when I felt totally alert, I'd switch the game into the spacial mode.

"Is there more to it than Sal?" Seldon asked, with perceptiveness that no longer surprised me.

"Yes," I said hesitantly. "But the worst of it all is that I don't really know exactly what's happening."

"I don't suppose you're worried about the weather?"

"No. I wish it were something you could help with."

Seldon made two shots and then missed. "The weather isn't the only thing I know about."

"Yeah?"

"That's right. I even know something about human nature."

"And what might that be?" I asked as I waited for room to make my shot.

"That it isn't healthy to brood for a long time. Sometimes you need to be able to share your problems."

"Share and share alike. Would you like a double helping?" I missed my shot and left him set up with three easy ones.

"I'm serious. If you want to talk, I'd be happy to listen."

I waited while I watched him sink the first two. "Suppose, just hypothetically, of course, that someone told you that at some point in your future, you would do something very much against your nature."

"How much faith do you put in this 'someone'? Is he an unimpeachable source, a reliable informant, or maybe a guy on recreational drugs?"

"The first."

"How explicit is he? Does he say you're going to die in your second century or does he say that in eight hundred and twenty-six days you'll stub your toe at fourteen hundred hours while getting out of the shower?"

"In between." What the hell. If the enforcers already knew it, what harm could there be if Seldon knew it? "Scapescope says that sometime between one and six weeks from now I'll commit a political crime."

He missed his shot. "What do *you* think about that?" he asked, looking at me, maybe to make sure I wasn't joking.

"Like I'm in a nightmare. What do you think? That's not my style, Seldon, you know that."

"I guess that explains Sal, too?"

"Right."

Seldon paused before he spoke. "How often does scapescope make mistakes about something like that?"

I explained about the entries being perfectly clear, and the implications. My words faltered briefly as an enforcer started a game at an adjacent table.

"Exactly what is it that you are going to do?" he asked.

"That's *maybe* 'going to do.' I don't know. That list covers a relatively wide range of choices."

While I was talking, he sank the last ball. The table tallied the score and reset the balls into starting position. Seldon placed his stick on the cue ball image and moved it to his usual point. He broke them and the sound effects clattered loudly. He looked thoughtful as he walked around the table.

"You know," he began. "Sometimes we come across a weather system that's so large that we can't eliminate it entirely. But advance warning gives us a chance to prepare for it. That warning allows us to do what we can to minimize its size and enables us to endure the conditions a little better when the storm finally culminates."

I looked at my next shot. "Yes, I suppose that works with weather. I'm not too sure about how it works with crime."

"With weather it helps to know all the factors—why pressure builds, why humidity increases, all the physical laws and theories. If a person's aware of the variables and tries to minimize the critical ones, he stands a better chance. And the more advance warning he gets, the more effective he can be when he works on the various causes."

"I guess that sounds reasonable. And if this person doesn't even know what the factors are, he can at least use that lead time to investigate the possibilities."

"Right." Seldon sank another ball. "Look, Mike, I know this wasn't much help. I'm sure that's what you've already planned to do. But if you need some moral support, I'm always around."

"You're doing really well already. Thanks." He had helped. I didn't feel nearly so alone as when I had come in. We played a few more games and he beat me consistently. I gave up and said good night.

The boost Seldon had given me didn't start eroding for another couple of days. Sometime after midnight I woke up bathed in sweat. My apartment must have been up to 45 degrees Celsius.

I fumbled around and located the thermostat. It was

set for a cool 18 degrees and said it was currently 43.
Great. Not knowing what to do, I tapped it lightly. I
stepped up on a chair, where I could feel the heat ex-
changer. After a moment it began to feel cooler to the
touch.

I went back to bed and thought of Sal until the temperature finally felt more comfortable, and I went to
sleep.

Probably no more than a half hour later I was awake
again, shivering and freezing. It had been a long time
since I had seen my breath. I tapped the thermostat
again, but didn't dare put my hand on the heat ex-
changer this time. I did call air-conditioning, and they
said they'd investigate immediately. For ten minutes I
stood in my open doorway to stay warm.

Gradually the temperature rose, and I went back to
bed feeling that the problem was solved. By the time I
had to leave for work, four more hot/cold cycles had
come and gone, and I was thoroughly angry once again.

It only made matters worse when I arrived at my office, checked my calls, and found that the highest priority message was a summons to Arthur's office.

chapter
FOUR

As I made the journey to Arthur's office I wondered what had prompted his call. Resentment flared. Why couldn't he simply call on the phone and say something like, "Hi, Mike. Can you please come up when you get a chance so we can discuss something or other?"

It wouldn't be quite so annoying if he even called *some* of the time. His expressions were hard to read, but on the phone I could at least try to gauge the tone of his voice and make a wild guess based on the depth of his frown. But no, he had to send text messages, or have Rob send them. Maybe Arthur treated some of his other subordinates better than this. If we were all subjected to the same irritations, there probably would have been a payroll deduction for going-away gifts.

Rob greeted me with a cheerful smile when I got to Arthur's office. As usual, during the subservience-emphasis delay I didn't feel talkative, so I waited silently. Despite my mood I grinned at a couple of Rob's graffiti choices for the day. The first one proclaimed, "Telepathy is all in your mind." The second read, "Precognition is an idea ahead of its time.'' The last two escaped me though. ''Michael Dunn was a dwarf star,'' might have made sense if I had known who he was, but I didn't ask. ''Beware of proctologists with the hiccups,'' made no more sense. Either I was falling behind in current events, or Rob's trivia inclination was showing.

My mood lightened a bit and I held my temper until Arthur called me. This time I waited for him to speak. I was as tense as a fly with eyestrain.

Maybe Arthur's basic problem was that he had been promoted above his competency level. I had heard that he was at least a moderately good engineer before. Perhaps the frustrations of having a higher-prestige job but not having the skills to perform it adequately were grating on him, so he took it out on the only people he could: his subordinates. Then again, he might simply have been a jerk.

''Hello, Mike.'' Arthur swept some imaginary dust off the glossy black desk top.

''Hello.'' I tried to keep my voice neutral.

''Do you recall the urgent message I sent you yesterday?''

''Yes, I do.''

''Do you remember the subject?'' Arthur rarely passed up a chance for a good game of autocrat and mouse.

''It's been less than twenty-four hours. Certainly I remember it. You asked for a progress report on the Kipple lens project.''

''Mike,'' he said, pausing for effect. ''I think that it is imperative that we understand each other.''

''So far, I think we do.'' There was no way to speed him up.

''Until recently I was under that same impression. But I guess we all realize that first impressions aren't always accurate." He waited for me to reply.

"I hardly think a half year of diligent work qualifies as a first impression. But what's more important, why do you imply that it might be an incorrect impression? Haven't you got over that mix-up with the monthly report yet?"

"I'm not very pleased with your performance on that task, but this little chat is not due to the monthly report."

"To what do I owe the honor, then?"

"Don't be flippant with me, young man."

Young man. He might have been all of five years my senior. Holding my temper became a bigger effort. "Sorry. I'm just getting a little impatient. Have I done something wrong?"

"Surely that is obvious by now. I asked you if you remembered the priority request that I gave you yesterday. You admitted it, therefore you must have received my message. Consequently you have no excuse for failing to deliver that report."

"But I *didn't* fail to deliver it. I sent you that report yesterday before lunch." The sinking feeling I had experienced the last time I was in his office returned and was fast turning into a stinking feeling. What was happening?

"Your claim is hard to support. I never received the report."

I couldn't afford to call him a liar or a fool, so I asked, "Would you mind if I took a look at the log?"

"Help yourself." He didn't act as if he felt insulted. As smug as a thug on a drug.

His response wasn't encouraging. He popped out a screen and pointed it toward me. With a few keywords he displayed yesterday's recorded log from 0900 through 1530. The entries were all clear—and all from other people, or automatically generated.

"I'm at a total loss, Arthur. I sent you that report yesterday morning, and I was very careful."

"I think the only thing around here that is at a total loss is my misplaced faith in you. Mike, you are simply going to have to force yourself to become more conscientious."

We had been over this same ground before, real stomping ground. I realized that my fingers were wrapped around the arms of the chair. They hurt. I took a few deep breaths, convinced that if I spoke out, I'd let all the anger show. After another moment I felt more in control.

"I really do think there's been some mistake—"

"I concur. I think you may be performing at a level lower than I had hoped for a person in your position. I think, for the time being, there should be a closer match between your performance and your grade. Let's see," he said, looking at his screen. "You're currently a fifty-six. Fifty-two seems to be a more appropriate level. At least that won't affect any of your basic privileges. And, by the way, you need to work on your punctuality. You've been late two days in the last two weeks. I hope this impresses upon you the need for diligence. That will be all."

I couldn't speak or move. A four-level demotion. For a mistake. He had the authority to bump me up or down ten levels, but that option was exercised about as frequently as new elements were discovered. I rose to leave, not daring to say anything for fear that my rage would be audible and cost me the other six levels.

"Oh," he added quietly, "have that report to me very soon, won't you, Mike?"

I think I managed to nod. Totally ignoring Rob, I

strode out to the hall and, as hard as I could, rammed my hand against the wall. That stupid jerk!

By the time I arrived at my office, my mind had cleared some, but the anger still burned. I collapsed tiredly into my chair and slowly collected my strength.

Before starting to reconstruct the Kipple report, I had to check one forecast. Several scapescope menus flashed by as the data went deeper and deeper. Dubiously I scanned the list that filled the screen after my last request.

Damn! Seeing my name there wasn't much easier to take than seeing my name on the criminal list. This list was pending GS-level demotions. Less than one week uptime.

The second digit of my new rating was illegible, but the first one was very clear. It was a four.

What was in store for me? More of the same? I still had no clues as to Arthur's recent overreactions or how the mix-ups might have occurred.

Thinking of Arthur reminded me of the Kipple report. I'd better get it to him quickly. Within moments I had retrieved it and was looking at the first page displayed on my screen. I used audio commands since my hand still hurt. A brief examination of the rest of the text showed that it was complete and was the final draft.

This time when I sent it, I called Rob for verification. I stayed on the line until he had not only verified its arrival, but also printed a hard copy. The note of sympathy in his voice helped me fight the paranoia.

My problem now was lack of expert knowledge. If I were going to have any luck in trying to find out more about my fate, I needed to know more about a vital subject: law enforcement.

I wished that Sal had been more communicative

about her job. Vacillating for a moment, I told the phone her ID. She answered a moment later, from work.

Her frowning was visible for less than five seconds.

"I'm sorry," she said. "I can't talk." And she switched off.

I called again. That call was even shorter. On my third call I had time to say, "I'll keep at it."

She stayed on the line when I called the fourth time. We both knew that she could have set her unit to reject calls from my phone, but I could have called from any office phone.

"Please, Mike. Make it fast. I can't afford this."

"I need information. Nothing sensitive. Help me for ten minutes, and I'll leave you alone."

She hesitated, probably thinking about how persistent I could be when I wanted something badly enough. "Ten minutes. One time only?"

"Guaranteed."

"You'd better be telling me the truth. I'll meet you at your place in fifteen minutes." Already it was *my* place.

"Right."

She was waiting for me when I arrived. I hadn't cleared her thumbprint from the lock. Her frown was more emphatic in person than it was on the video.

Sal was maybe ten centimeters shorter than I, but she was standing so stiffly upright that our eyes were almost level. Evidently she found it hard to meet my gaze. She rubbed the back of her neck with her hand. So she was nervous, and maybe not callous enough to avoid feeling guilty. If I hadn't known her quite so well, I would have tried again to persuade her that she was doing the wrong thing.

"Let's get one thing straight," she said, "before anything else happens. I cannot take chances with my career. I came because it was obvious that you would keep calling until you got results. And for the benefit of any bugs, I know you'll be on the criminal list and I want no part of it. You've got ten minutes to ask your questions, but I won't discuss anything confidential."

"Dammit, Sal. I hardly know what questions to ask. But thanks for coming at least."

"You'd better start." If love is blind, Sal was near-sighted, at best.

"Okay, okay." I scratched my head. "So I'll be on the political criminal list. That's all I know. How can I find out exactly what my crime is going to be?"

"You can't, at least not without enforcer clearances. You can get to general statistics and, I guess, the first-level descriptions by cross-indexing the summaries that are available to engineers. But you can't get access to any restricted data, which includes almost everything else." She must have seen my expression, because she added, "No way. I won't give you any information you don't have the authorization to have. Even if I knew."

The implication that the detailed lists didn't tell much more was interesting. Maybe not informative, but puzzling.

"So the nature of the offense isn't visible yet?"

"Infer what you want. I can't say."

"What types of potential offenses rate personal sur-veillance?"

"You mean you're actually being followed?"

"Yes."

"Well, there aren't consistent rules." She looked more worried. "That's not exactly news to be happy about, though."

"Nice. How much advance warning will enforcement

get when—you know, when I do it?''

"Mike, I don't know. You're asking hard questions.''

"Okay. Just one more. You know me pretty well, Sal. Do you really think I'm likely to commit this crime, whatever it is?''

"Oh, for— I don't know. I don't know what the crime is or anything about what pressures you might go through before you get to that point.''

"You don't think the situation with us is producing pressure?''

"I'm sorry, Mike. I've got to go. I hope you make it, but I can't do this again.'' Sal's eyes met mine briefly before she turned to go.

I knew then that I wouldn't call her again. I hadn't learned much. In retrospect, perhaps I hadn't expected to. Maybe I had just wanted to see her again to be sure of how she felt.

As she closed the door I was subliminally aware of her trim figure. She was so weight-conscious that she wouldn't step on a scale when her hair was wet. I forced my thoughts to other topics.

The end of the dayshift was nearing, but I went back to the office to see if I could learn any more from scapescope. Fortunately Arthur hadn't checked on me while I was out.

Before starting again, I checked my transmission log. The absence of entries in Arthur's log still bothered me. My brief examination gave consistent but disturbing information.

My record showed no indication of any transmissions yesterday morning.

I didn't understand, so I dropped the subject for the time being. I turned my attention back to scapescope, but I didn't know what areas of information might be helpful in my search. I roamed through various menus haphazardly, my path occasionally altered by minor skirmishes between my subconscious and my conscious mind.

My voice got tired, so I switched to keyboard input. My fingers quit typing and I examined the display occupying the screen. It showed the breakdown of predicted crimes by category. My specialty, political crimes, was an elite. It encompassed less than one percent of the total. I supposed that made sense. With scapescope around, planned activities were much harder to accomplish than spur-of-the-moment crimes.

Still, being a member of an elite failed to fill me with pride. Life as a recluse would give me more esprit de corps.

I flipped on the computer. Taking it out of local mode to get access to public-domain data, I called up a summary of types of crime sorted by enforcement office responsible for prevention and apprehension. Political crime had its own dedicated PA office.

I wished that my terminal had the same access to non-public-domain information that their office had. Maybe I could dig out the reason that Arthur Springer was giving me such a hard time about two relatively painless mishaps. For that matter, maybe Arthur himself was responsible for them.

Perhaps he had deleted the Kipple report and altered his log. But no, even if he were clever enough to do that, it wouldn't explain how he acquired the first draft of my monthly report. What I most needed was broader permission for access to scapescope. Unfortunately it wasn't very likely that I would get it. Already there was widespread public dissatisfaction with the way information flowed. Scapescopes were intended to be restricted to job-related tasks, but information had ways of flowing uphill.

My investigation was curtailed by Harlan's arrival, which signified checkout time. There was a small chance that it was my imagination, but Harlan seemed measurably less friendly than usual. Who else was reading enforcer statistics?

After I left, I made a quick call to Seldon and arranged to meet him later. A light meal refreshed me, and I went up to the game room to look around for Seldon. The cubbyholed area was so large that it was hard to be entirely sure that he wasn't there yet, but I was probably the first one to arrive. I searched for something to occupy me until he came.

A card game seemed to be the best choice. I could leave it whenever I wanted to. I turned abruptly to walk back to that area and bumped squarely into an enforcer. Excusing myself, I hurried away, annoyed by the feeling that it was not a coincidence that he had been so close.

Once in the right area I easily found a vacant terminal. I keyed in my ID and volunteered my thumbprint. The game computer showed me a summary of games in progress and asked for my preference.

There was a slight delay until a round finished. I used the time to specify my options. My handicap would have been smaller if I were willing to make my identity known to the other participants, but I wanted to be able to drop out anytime I pleased. For variety, and because I felt lazy, I picked the summary option that gave a continual recap of cards previously played but cost me more handicap.

The round in progress must have ended, because the terminal displayed my hand being dealt. I checked my privacy by moving my head from side to side. Good.

The terminal kept the image visible unless I moved too fast.

The game started, and I lapsed into a mildly attentive state and adopted my defensive reflexes. A few hands later I was slightly down.

A glance behind me to look for Seldon got me down in a different direction. An enforcer was lounging about twenty meters away.

Several rounds later a hand clasped my shoulder. I turned and saw Seldon. I finished the round and signed off, noting that my account was credited with a small increase.

Seldon's favorite game was holopolo, so we edged our way to a vacant machine back in a corner. The last people using it had been playing slamball, but we switched it over and talked while we played.

"I bet you didn't realize," I said, "that you're playing with a GS-52 instead of a GS-56." I went on to explain the last day's activities.

"You sure don't mess around with just one problem at a time, do you?"

"No. Like I always say, if something's worth doing, it's worth doing thoroughly."

"Still no reason to explain why Arthur is reacting so violently?"

"For a while I worried that it might be the result of Cavantalo's third law of organizational momentum."

"Which says?"

"For every organizational action there will be an equal but opposite reaction. I've made suggestions that Arthur may resist. But that doesn't seem to be it. I'm beginning to worry less about Arthur. He's certainly not giving me any breaks, but I'm starting to think that he's just a symptom, not a cause. Seldon, you use computers a lot in meteorology. Do you have frequent problems?"

"Nothing like this. All new systems seem to have a few problems that have to be worked out by trial and error, but the basic communications and editing systems have been around long enough to be pretty thoroughly tested. Are they trying out any system upgrades in your area?"

"No. That was one thing I wondered about, but I've been paying attention to the release number every time I use the system. It's always the same, and it's the one we've been using for at least the past year or two."

"I don't know. There must be an explanation, but it's not obvious to me."

We played for another hour before quitting. Seldon provided another large dose of moral support, but we weren't able to answer any burning questions.

Each time I thought about being on the political criminal list, I grew more nervous. Penalties were computed by multiplying three factors: the potential for harm to the individual, the number of people affected, and the probability of success. What that meant for the political crimes division was that even if the harm to an individual was small and the probability of success was low, multiplying them by a potentially astronomical number of people affected yielded a huge penalty.

In increasing order, the penalties were a fine, confinement, physical punishment, nightmare treatment, reprogramming, and death. The idea of transforming my mind into a vegetable turned me cold. I didn't want to die, but that might be preferable to the "vegematic."

The next day was fairly routine except for the dunning notice. Somehow my rent payment had been lost on its way from my account to the government's. It must have taken me two hours on the phone to straighten it out. I never did find out exactly what had gone wrong, but everyone I talked to seemed to think the situation was rectified by the time I finished.

Several more days passed as I struggled for answers. I began to feel that I had no more control over my life than did a bowling pin. Okay, I'm in position now, Arthur. You can roll another one. I wasn't able to resolve any significant inconsistencies, but the more time I spent thinking and investigating, the more I became convinced that I had been suppressing an extremely unpleasant explanation.

Unlikely as it seemed, the most reasonable rationale for the recent happenings was the possibility that I was being deliberately manipulated.

Once I admitted it to myself, the questions that arose were: By whom? And for what purpose?

chapter
FIVE

In spite of being convinced that manipulation was the only logical explanation for recent events, I could think of absolutely nothing that would explain *why* it might be happening. I reached that conclusion just before quitting time. A strong case of mental fatigue convinced me to table the matter temporarily.

Maybe if my subconscious chewed on it for a while, it would be a more digestible size the next day. If a little knowledge was dangerous, I was absolutely deadly then.

A light meal at the cafeteria filled me, and I went back to my apartment to try to relax. Lately the room had seemed smaller every time I examined it, which was a little funny; I would have thought that my office was the more claustrophobic of the two rooms. Perhaps it was about time for refresher conditioning.

My examination of the cubicle was brief—there wasn't much to see. The desk and bed were behind mirrors, invisibly folded into the wall, as were the chairs and speakers. The wall screen was set to show a forest scene, with an insert that displayed date, time, and pending appointments. There were none. The only belongings that made this place unique to me were stored in my closet, in my computer, or on a small, concealed shelf, along with my portable terminal. The ceiling itself was a heat-exchanging plate that controlled the temperature, which was currently a cool 18 degrees Celsius. Small vents carried fresh air.

For a moment I could imagine that I was inside a well-lighted, beige-colored coffin, the interior marred only by a wall mural and mirrors. Then the feeling passed and the image of the room coalesced into the familiar.

I scanned my to-do list to see if there was anything interesting. There was. Pat's letter was still unanswered. Settling back with my portable terminal, I decided to enjoy myself, so I entered requests for about two hours of music, mostly current, with a few classics scattered in. A modest royalty bill flashed on the screen.

Pat's letter consumed only half of the screen. I reread it, curious again about her current whereabouts. No clues. She had sent just the text—no visuals at all. I could have displayed her picture, but I chose to visualize her face.

My visualizations were usually flattering, although Pat didn't need enhancement. She had clear brown eyes and long brown hair that she almost had to brush out of her eyes.

At least I assumed she still wore her hair long. She hadn't sent any visuals during the last year or so.

I thought about telling her of my current misfortunes, but decided against it, hoping to know more by the next time I wrote. I mentioned the situation with Sal without explaining the background.

After that, I rambled for a while, recommending some new music, most of which was composed by humans. I mentioned a few new novels, all written by

humans—at any rate, they were advertised as being
authored by humans. The computer-written curiosities
that I had read so far were unsatisfying. They featured
large vocabulary and reasonably good diction but still
seemed to have paper characters with questionable motivations. Also you could guarantee that they contained
no food for thought, not even a snack.

I'd been enjoying the music while thinking about my
next response when suddenly the volume thundered past
my threshold of pain. I scrambled to turn it down as
quickly as I could, but my ears rang for the next ten
minutes. What was going on? I hadn't ever had this
many problems with technology. Several more minutes
passed before I calmed down enough to start thinking
about Pat's letter again.

Pat had not talked about any books or records lately,
so I wondered if she were still connected to the main net.
She liked her privacy, but I couldn't imagine that she
would find it important enough to forsake the newest
material.

I didn't envy her dilemma. She had strong negative
feelings about the size of Brother Sammy, but she found
quite a few of the benefits desirable. I sometimes
thought that she secretly wished that the arts were dis-
criminated against by the government, so she could be
free to dislike the system completely. As it was, she used
the available services grudgingly.

Pat had gone through a phase several years before.
She tried to make herself completely independent of the
government. A wristcomp could record and play back
only a few minutes of audio, so she bought an old
digital recorder. She could still enjoy music, but frequently succumbed to the urge to listen to new works.
So she tied in to the system to record original material.

She also decided to confine her reading to actual

physically bound literature. Lots of older volumes were still available on paper or plastic at almost reasonable prices, but once again she discovered a longing to read newly written pieces. So she returned to the public net rather than read nothing except products of the past.

The only arena in which she had a large degree of success was communications. She certainly found out who her close friends were when she quit answering her phone and expected all conversations to be in person. I felt relief when she finished the struggle and evidently conceded that at least some of the facilities weren't going to be easily displaced.

The whole experience never dampened her spirit, however. She always found a way to gain from a situation.

Just thinking of her determination and courage made me feel better. It was a long time since I had thought of her as an older sister. In a way I couldn't understand, my resolve strengthened. Maybe it was possible to keep fighting the problems, and perhaps even win. It wasn't until that moment that I realized how depressed I had been. Normally I could recover relatively quickly from disappointments, but this latest sequence of events was a good deal worse than my usual doses.

I finished the letter, adding an oblique attempt to thank her for the moral support. After keying in her blind-drop ID, I waited a few seconds before the acknowledgment came back, saying the way station had received it. From there, after a random delay to prevent Brother Sammy from easily tracing its path, it would be forwarded to Pat's drop, scrambled both for content and message length. The drop system also routinely transmitted dummy messages to all users of the system. My local terminal was set to ignore any message from it that didn't include a prearranged sequence.

Presently I realized that I was staring at a blank screen. The time seemed perfect for escape, so I gave instructions for the music to soften gradually and cut off thirty minutes after the last time I responded to hourly prompts. Then I went to bed.

At work the next morning my concentration was terrible. I had to finish an analysis and report for Arthur, but it was frequently necessary to drag my wandering attention back.

The evaluation concerned molecular recording techniques. There were three competing systems, and naturally each was praised by its sponsor and damned by the competitors. The Ramirvel technique seemed to be the easy winner because of its higher recording density and because all its sister technologies were healthy as far uptime as scapescope could see. On a clear day you could see whoever, whatever, wherever, whenever, whyever, and know where the funding came from.

I felt a little sympathy for Sandoval. Her analysis was more thorough, particularly in the area of computing loss factors and the projected life of the recording medium. But I had to be impartial. Ramirvel's method showed the best short-run promise, and we could always reevaluate it in a couple of years.

I spent more time trying to figure out who might have a reason to manipulate me than I spent working on the analysis, but it was finally done. Then I tried to anticipate all possible contingencies.

Once again I saved several copies of the final draft, each with a unique password. Finally satisfied that at least I wouldn't be caught in the same old traps, I called Arthur's office.

"Hello, Mike," Rob answered. "What can I do for

you?'' His ever-present grin was cheery.

"I've finished a recorder evaluation that I need to send up—but this time I want to be one hundred percent certain that it gets there okay."

"Sure. How do you want to go about it?" If Rob thought I was going crazy, he gave no sign. There was no sarcasm or condescension in his voice or expression. He simply seemed willing to do whatever I requested.

"First let me go ahead and transmit it." I punched the button as I spoke.

After a short delay Rob said, "All right. It's here."

"Okay, would you check your log?"

Another delay. "It's entered in the log."

"Now would you transmit your current display to my office?" My text screen filled up and showed Arthur's office log for the last three hours. I requested a hard copy and filed it. "Only one more request, Rob."

"Go ahead."

"Can you retrieve the first page of the text?"

"All set."

"Could you transmit that display?" He agreed, and I watched my screen fill with the text. A brief scan of the words convinced me that the report had been transmitted and recorded properly. Another touch of a button and a hard copy spewed out of the printer. I thanked him and signed off.

I felt silly as I sat there in my chair. To be consistent, I really should have furtively glanced behind me to make sure that no one had crept up on me while I was sitting in my tiny office. I was objective enough to realize that I was adopting some seemingly paranoid methods. There I was with multiple copies of my text, retransmitted text, and a copy of Arthur's log.

But I still could not find any possible explanation for the recent mix-ups except deliberate manipulation. They

simply couldn't be ordinary errors, on my part or anyone else's.

But who?

I tried again to imagine who might be responsible.
That was a borderline choice of words; I knew quite a
few responsible people, but none who might be *responsible*.

Past enemies? Not too likely. There were people with
whom I'd had disagreements, and people I just plain
didn't like, but I usually had a firm grip on my temper.
Besides, whoever was engineering the mistakes, if that
was what was happening, had to have very specialized
knowledge and clearances to get that deep into the system. I couldn't remember any even casual clashes with
someone with those qualifications. Now that I thought
about it, I wasn't sure that I even *knew* anyone with
those talents.

So if personal revenge was out, what was left? Who
would gain at my expense? This didn't seem to be the
work of someone with an overdeveloped sense of competition; to excel in the GS, you needed only to be diligent, eager, and moderately intelligent. And if someone
were rigging these mishaps, I didn't have any criticisms
about intelligence.

What was left? Maybe it wasn't work-related. Perhaps someone was interested in Sal. Not to slight Sal,
but so far I had the feeling that the whole scheme must
be above the level of personalities. Plus I hadn't seen
any indications of someone trying to ask her out, besides Arthur. And he didn't have the resources to do
this.

One by one I discarded the possibilities that came
to me. It was time to put my subconscious back to
work. But before I left the office, one unpleasant task
remained; I probably shouldn't have, but part of me

insisted upon turning on scapescope. Several displays popped up, replaced in turn by the following displays. When they stopped, the last one showed demotions and corresponding new GS levels for the next few days.

The first digit, a four, was still clearly visible next to my name. And it was there as early as two days uptime. I felt as frustrated as someone who's been told he's not qualified to get his first job because he doesn't have any experience. I had to get out of the office.

The game room at first seemed like a good idea after dinner, but I wasn't in the mood. What seemed like a better idea was to find out about my air-conditioning problems a few nights back. The incident bothered me more and more the longer I thought about it.

I found out where the office in charge was, and I reluctantly took an elevator down to the minus-two level. The door opened onto an immense work area. An incredible array of bulky gray machines stretched into the distance. The level was so large that in the distance the ceiling support columns seemed to converge into a solid wall forming a viewing horizon.

A blue slidewalk took me to the office I wanted. I could have called, but my paranoia was extending to new limits.

It was a brief and frustrating visit. Not only did they say that such an occurrence was almost unheard of; they said mine was literally unheard of. Their records showed no complaint call from me and indicated a constant, comfortable 18 degrees Celsius in my apartment for the last month.

That was enough for me for the day, so I went back home. Maybe reading would take my mind off the situation. The frustration had built up to the point where I felt as if I'd go berserk if I kept thinking about it all the time.

It had been a while since I listed the current offerings, so I had the computer scan my list of favorite authors and identify any works copyrighted in the last six months. (Most authors were major or devoted or both, because with scapescope budding novelists often dropped out as soon as it was obvious that they would not be an instantaneous success.)

There were a few new editions of *Popular Photonics*, but that night I needed some fiction, preferably escapist, so I picked a mystery from the list and watched as the royalty charges were made. As the first page came up on my screen, I settled in for an evening that might take me away from my troubles.

In retrospect, I was fortunate to be able to tune out for a while. The next day brought new pressures to grin and bear.

On my arrival at the office I found two messages awaiting me. One was a notice that I was due for a medical exam. The second was another summons to Arthur's office.

chapter
SIX

The latest summons was as puzzling as it was annoying. There was no way that Arthur could find fault with my recorder evaluation. Riding up to his office, I clenched backup hard copies of my log. This time I had my proof. No mix-ups, no missing reports, no first drafts.

So why then was I also convinced that this meeting would be a disaster?

Optimism and pessimism battled each other and kept me off balance. I could still see the four that was likely to be the first digit of my new rating, and I felt the tension in my hand that gripped the papers. I switched hands to relieve the discomfort, but my fingers still didn't relax.

I reviewed my precautions to make sure he couldn't complain about this one. Everything should be covered. The knots and rumbling in my stomach told me that my body wasn't in total agreement with my brain.

"You're still sure I sent in that recorder report?" I asked Rob when I reached the office.

"Absolutely." Rob's eyes told me just as surely as his

response that it was so. At least I had an ally, in case I needed one.

Arthur called me in before my patience ran out. For once he came directly to the point.

"I read the evaluation you completed yesterday. Not only do I not appreciate the criticisms of me; I don't believe you'll find very many people receptive to criticisms of the government. I must say that I am thoroughly disappointed, though not very surprised."

I was dumbfounded. I was confused, irritated, and worried. "Criticisms, Arthur?" was all I could say.

"Dammit! I am intolerably tired of your blasé attitude, and I am totally unamused by your damn faked forgetfulness. And I'm tired of excuses. When I give you a job to do, I expect you to complete it with a professional attitude. No procrastination and no lies. Do you understand me?"

I still hadn't found a response. It was just as well, because he quickly made it obvious that the question was merely rhetorical. He hardly slowed down as he continued.

"You know, I just do not understand young people today. A prank like this will not be condoned. It is not a simple case of thoughtless disregard for a superior. You are wasting my time and your time, and you are wasting government funds. You cannot laugh this one off, young man."

I certainly wasn't laughing. Of all the people I knew, I probably valued Arthur's opinions the least, but he *was* my boss. And that gave him a good deal more leverage than I cared for. And that was definitely not a good deal. But I still had no idea what had gone wrong this time.

"Arthur, would you slow down? You're way ahead of me—I don't now what you're talking about."

"Dammit, I have had enough. Just admit your responsibility and get back to your office."

"Responsibility for what? I haven't done anything wrong."

"We obviously do not share a common set of values, then."

"Arthur, just tell me what you think I did. Then I'll tell you if I did it and if I enjoyed it, all right?"

"Don't take that tone with me. And you already know damn well what you did."

"Well, then, would you tell me your view of it?"

He finally paused for a moment. I pressed again. "Tell me what you think I did." He wavered for another few seconds, and then turned on the wall screen, anger making his economical motions more jerky than ever.

He punched a few more keys, and my evaluation appeared in large letters. The tightening in my chest relaxed a bit as I noticed that the text appeared unaltered. Once the conversation subsided, I had more opportunity to think, but there was still no clue to tell me where to direct my thoughts.

Arthur scrolled through the text and slowed when he neared the last screenful. My head started throbbing as I noticed some paragraphs that I didn't remember placing there. And I had brought copies of only the first page.

Reading the first few words, I decided that I would be much happier if Arthur didn't read to me, but he was already starting. "This is one of my favorites. 'One conclusion pointed to by this summary is that a great deal of money has been wasted just by evaluating products this late in their development cycle.' My God, Mike. If you see problems with the way we do business, make your suggestions in more conventional channels. You hardly need to tell the whole world."

"But that's not my writing—there's been another foul-up."

"I agree with the second part of your sentence. Oh, and how about this," he said, scrolling to the final page. " 'It is also reasonable to point out that the weak link in the whole chain of activities is Arthur Springer. His bottlenecking, pompous, and insensitive techniques are a handicap that must be experienced to be fully appreciated. The astute observer will also be stunned by his degree of incompetence.' Need I say more? There was absolutely no call to write things like this. Even if you believed them, you should at least have the decency to bring them up with me first, in private."

"But I didn't. This is all new to me—that's the honest truth." At least I didn't *write* them.

"Dammit, quit lying to me. Rob told me all about your phony precautions yesterday."

"Rob said they were phony?" I asked, wondering how many people were choosing sides.

"No, you've got him fooled. But I'm a little smarter."

If brains were money, he wouldn't be able to tip for a breakfast, but I decided not to tell him that just yet. There was not the faintest trace of doubt that someone was setting me up, framing me. I wasn't very optimistic that Arthur would believe me, but I had to try to tell him.

"This may be very hard for you to accept, but I did not place those lines of text in the report. Someone is trying, and damn near succeeding, to discredit me." Damn *near*? Did I say that?

"I think you should get out of my office right now, before I get even more angry. I'm not a schoolboy any longer." Arthur's eyes squinted still more, and I thought I could hear his breathing.

"It's the truth!"

"Do I look that gullible? Don't tell me—the paranoids are after you."

"Arthur, I did not accidentally send you the first draft of my monthly report. I didn't forget to send you that report that conveniently disappeared. And I most certainly did not write those criticisms. Someone has been intercepting my transmissions, or they have access to both of our data bases."

"Mike, does the number 'forty-eight' mean anything to you?"

It sure did. It was fifty-two minus another four. "You can't demote me again. This isn't my doing."

" 'Can't' isn't a word you may use to describe my capabilities. I'll do anything I please, as long as it's within my authorized activities. I would take the whole six right now, but I'd like to retain a bit of a threat."

He might as well have dropped me to a forty-six. The other two levels seemed negligible compared to the eight I had already lost. The stress was mounting, and I found it hard to think clearly.

". . . leave now," I heard him say.

"What?"

"I said, 'I think you'd better leave now.' And I suggest that you think up a better excuse for the next time you're in here."

Partially dazed, I rose and prepared to leave. He always liked to have the last word, but I guess he forgot that he already had. "Mike, I think you might want to start exploring the possibility of a career on the outside." Outside the GS, he meant.

Imagining another onslaught, I didn't reply. I went back to my office and sat for a long time. The shock gradually subsided to a level at which I was able to think more coherently. Along with the clarity of thought came the anger.

Someone would pay.

All of my lingering doubts about the source of my troubles were swept clean. There was absolutely no way

I could call any of the recent events accidents. Someone was deliberately, calculatingly rigging them.

The same old questions reared their heads once again, but this time I knew that I could take them 100 percent seriously. Why me? And for what purpose?

I had worked on those questions before, both consciously and subconsciously, but still had not arrived at any remote possibilities. Arthur's interpretation of the happenings bothered me a lot, but I had to admit that it was in character for him. An argument with him was about as useful to me as a Swedish–Swahili dictionary. He almost never stood up for his subordinates, probably thinking that the responsibility of support extended in only one direction. If he were behind the manipulation, then I might as well have puppet threads tied to my arms and legs. No, it had to be someone a lot smarter.

Once I thought about it, I also realized that the likelihood of my being bugged was now a certainty. Whoever put those criticisms of Arthur into my report was right on target. I had told Arthur truthfully that I had nothing to do with their appearance in the report, but I didn't tell him that the comments expressed my feelings reasonably well.

There was no point in searching my clothing or office for monitors. Even if they were using a physical plant rather than long-range detectors, it would be so small that I'd be wasting my time. In the unlikely event that I should find one, there wouldn't be any guarantee that there weren't twenty more on me, or that the next time I went out in public someone wouldn't simply drop several more into my hair.

So what could I do? Before starting to investigate, I felt a compulsion to find out more about my personal situation. I hate novel and cinema spoilers as much as anyone, but I had to know how this was going to come out, at least as far as I could see with scapescope.

Several menus flashed past, and I arrived at the critical section: the one that showed GS demotions and promotions. There wasn't much need to search the promotion list. When I found my name, my stomach felt worse than it did during a high-speed chute descent.

I almost wished I hadn't looked. The news was even worse than what I'd expected.

Sometime during the next week, my GS rating would change to zero, meaning that I would no longer be an employee of Brother Sammy.

On the good side, if there were such a thing, knowing that I was going to be fired for sure gave me freedom to choose among a wider range of possible actions. After all, what could it cost me?

After thinking about it for a while longer, I started getting confused. Maybe the knowledge that I was going to be fired anyway would guarantee that I would take some rash action that could force that result.

I didn't know whether the chicken or the other side of the road came first. Cause and effect. Because and expect. The old Heisenberg Uncertainty Principle—since the act of observing was enough to change the outcome, who could say what would have happened without the observer being in the loop?

I finally decided that it didn't matter. All I could do was try to determine who and why. Later the time might come to ask, "What next?"

Curiosity drove me to retrieve the uptime crimes list. The letters in the header and the body of the text informed me that within two weeks I would make the team.

Partly to continue my investigation and partly to divert my thoughts, I brought up the crime classification display. I had been staring at it but not reading for thirty seconds or so when the text was displaced by the system message that had shown up a couple of weeks before: "Update in progress—please try later."

Absentmindedly surprised, I moved on, but only moments later it happened again. Irritation began to get the better of curiosity. Some brief experimentation showed me that, in general, the affected area centered on access to enforcer-related statistics. My optimistic thought was that for some reason the enforcer branch was housecleaning, reorganizing, and performing a thorough update.

My pessimistic thought was that someone was locking me out.

Pessimism won. I was so discouraged that I quit for the day and went back to my apartment. At times like this I wished I would inherit a huge sum from a long-lost relative and could retire.

Except for the fact that there were hardly any inheritances of vast amounts. Not with scapescope. Typically, as soon as anyone found out that he was going to die in the next few months, whatever vast sums existed were quickly turned to less than half vast. Currently there was a movement to declare a person legally dead as soon as the death was predicted by scapescope.

The next day dragged by much too slowly. In a way it felt good to be employed still, but the knowledge of things to come was immensely frustrating.

Knowing that all too soon I'd be on my own, I made an appointment to get the medical exam I'd been notified of. A long lunch break left ample time for the checkup.

At the medical center a cigarette-smoking aide led me into a scanning room lined with electronic and photonic equipment. He and two others ran me through the testing sequence as device after device gathered data about various parts of my body. After a whirlwind analysis they left me in the lobby while the aide went to examine the results. Next to ads for special offers, a wall screen proclaimed, "A fool and his tonsils are soon parted."

The aide was out moments later, agitated and excited. "Mr. Cavantalo, would you come with me, please?"

"Why? What's wrong?"

"I'll tell you as we go. It's nothing to be alarmed about. The analysis has shown a small tumor near your lungs. We need to get it out, but you'll be up and around in no time at all."

I was starting to get alarmed.

"Do you work near high-radiation fields?" he asked as we walked.

"No, high-stress."

"What?"

"Nothing. Look, how sure are you that this tumor is really there?"

"You're not making sense, Mr. Cavantalo. The analysis *says* it's there."

I felt an almost overpowering sense of déjà vu. Something had to be wrong. "I'm not going to have an operation until I've talked with a doctor."

It was a long argument. He was emphatic about the need for speed, and I wouldn't move. Finally, apparently realizing that I wasn't going to give in, he summoned a doctor.

"What's this about your not wanting an operation?" the doctor asked. She was a short and determined person who had obviously dealt with recalcitrant patients before.

"This is going to be difficult to accept, but a—a friend of mine is a determined practical joker. And he's intimately familiar with hospital computer systems." I was stretching things quite a bit, but there didn't seem to be any other choice. "I won't believe there's a tumor there until you personally check it out—externally."

She didn't seem convinced, so I added, "And if you

find it, I'll give you a hundred credits. That's how sure I am.''

I didn't know if the offer swayed her or if she decided to humor me as long as I was so insistent, but she took me into another room and had me lie down on still another table while a huge device traveled over me on rails, and she intently watched a screen in the corner. The device stopped directly over where I assumed the "tumor" was, and then slid side-to-side several times. She asked me to roll slightly to different positions.

Finally the device slid to one end of its tracks, and she told me I could get up.

"Mr. Cavantalo, I—I think your friend has a despicable sense of humor. You can go now. There's no tumor. I'm sorry.''

"It's not your fault. Thanks.''

"Before you go, though, what's his name? Your friend's name?''

"I'm sorry, too, Doctor. I don't know.''

I went back to work, angry as well as sorry. Investigation took on an even higher priority for me.

I came to the disturbing conclusion that at least a limited information blockage did exist. The "update in progress" messages didn't go away. I might have tried sneaking into someone else's office to use a different terminal, if I had any idea of what good it might do me. For all I knew, the blockage existed just to frustrate me, and not to keep me from actually learning something of value.

I spent a little time trying to think of something I would be able to do on the outside, but I didn't actually give it any serious thought. All the scapescopes were rigidly controlled by Brother Sammy. No one on the outside had any direct access.

One thought kept coming back to me: Arthur had to be the person to make the decision that would sever my connection with the government. He wouldn't be able to take that action on his own, but he could recommend it to the board. Therefore, Arthur was the person I needed to convince.

Even without the foreknowledge of my dismissal, I would not have felt optimistic about being able to change his mind about anything more important than where your lap goes when you stand up. But I had to try.

To that end I started making hard copies of everything I could think of that had any chance of supporting my case. If I hadn't been so worried and frustrated, I might have seen a bit of humor in the situation. With the advent of scapescope, large-scale gambling had died a rapid death, yet here I was, gambling on my ability to persuade Arthur that one of his beliefs wasn't true.

I found that, in spite of knowing the outcome, I still had to try. Apparently there's nothing like having your back up against the wall to help you straighten up your back.

I was about eighty percent impatient to talk to Arthur and twenty percent afraid that the conversation could be the final trigger, but I went up to his office and told Rob that I would wait there until Arthur would see me.

Naturally the wait was even longer than the wait after an appointment summons. If you ranked people according to the length of time you had to wait for them, Arthur would have an excellent score. If you ordered them by how much they were worth waiting for, the list would look a lot different. All things are numbing to him who waits.

Rob's graffiti selections occupied my thoughts briefly. "Telepathy means never having to say . . ." headed the list, followed by, "Mathematicians use the algorithm method." The last, "Every cloud has a silver iodide lining," I'd have to remember to pass on to

Seldon, but I didn't know if they still used the stuff.

Another item shared the wall screen with the graffiti. It was a copy of a news article, headlined by, "Hard Work Makes You Live Longer." At the bottom of the page, in bold strokes, someone had written, "Let's get busy, you people." Below that, in a different hand, another person had added, "You won't really live longer. It will just seem like it."

I could have tied my wristcomp into the central net to occupy myself, but the tiny keys were so inconvenient compared to my office and home terminals that I didn't bother. It wouldn't have surprised me to learn that Arthur had a blood-temperature sensor installed in the outer office. He called just as my temperature passed simmer and headed for boil.

"What do you want, Mike?" he asked once I was seated. Not "What can I do for you?" or any of a variety of less stress-producing salutations.

"I'd like to talk to you about my recent performance."

"It's about time. Are you finally going to explain what it is that you are trying to accomplish?"

"You've still got it all wrong. This isn't a confession or anything of the sort. Someone is behind this. Someone is responsible for these tricks, and it isn't me."

"Mike, I don't have the time or patience to listen to this same old garbage."

I agreed with him about the patience, but I pressed on. "It's not garbage. I've spent most of the last couple of days collecting evidence that I want you to look—"

"You have what? You spent even more of the government's time on this stupid pretense? I think you'd better return to your office and keep yourself very busy with legitimate work. That will be all."

"But, Arthur, I'm serious. I—"

"Get out!"

"Dammit! Open up your tiny little mind and—" The rage suddenly blossomed on his face, and I knew that I'd better leave—fast.

That pompous ass. I was so angry that I didn't remember anything of the trip back to my office. After a while I just realized that I was there. I didn't know what to do next, but I did know that I certainly wasn't going to accomplish any useful work soon.

I sat and boiled. I was overheating and had no way to vent the steam. If only there were a target. Arthur was acting the total bastard about the whole business, but he couldn't be responsible for anything more than seeing the worst side of it all. There had to be someone else.

But now wasn't the time to think it through. To do that I needed to be rational, cool, calm, collected, logical. Just then I was very close to zero for five. Zero for six, if you counted optimistic.

I spent several hours shuttling around on slidewalks and walking in some of the older sections of the complex. Occasionally I would become aware of my surroundings and make a conscious decision about what direction to go next.

My disorderly stream of thoughts slowly turned to a trickle. Temporarily brain-damaged, I realized that it was well after dinnertime. I had no appetite, so I skipped the meal and went back to the game room. I couldn't handle going home.

I knew what I wanted to do. No cards or holopolo tonight. Tonight it would be a total-immersion game.

There were two choices when I got there. A supersub and an avenger were free. I picked the avenger mainly for its destructiveness. A good catharsis might help.

Once I was inside, the lights dimmed gradually while I slipped into the harness. The option list came up, and I began my selection. The simulator itself would be my opponent this time. I'd had enough human competition for one day.

At the moment I felt a strong desire to thrash the devil out of whatever opponents the machine created, so I requested a huge supply of ordnance and field protection. The lights faded still more and my environment came into view.

As every time before, the location was new and unique. This one was patterned very roughly after the asteroid belt but had some significant differences. In this model the bodies were much closer together than in the real belt. The ratio of body diameters to the spacing between objects appeared to be about one to ten.

Also the relative velocities of the rocks were minimal. They reminded me of an old image of an underwater mine field.

It presented a few more choices, and I picked an eighty percent computer-assist. Tonight I wanted to pull a trigger without being bogged down with a full complement of high-speed reflex requirements. The ten-second countdown started. My feet found the pedals and I gripped the joystick tightly.

The timer ran out, the status display took its place, and the battle was on. Silently I edged the craft forward and to port. Within a minute one of the enemy had taken a shot at me from behind a small asteroid. I cranked up my beam intensity so high that I destroyed not only the enemy but the asteroid as well. The console computer warned me about energy limits, and the fight continued.

When the lights came back up, I could hardly believe that the entire hour had passed. I was sore where the straps had pulled on me to simulate acceleration. My body was damp from perspiration, despite the coolness of the air. The constant vigilance and tension had tired me.

But I felt good. I didn't bother to look at the score sheet that had tallied my performance indices. It summarized my score, kill ratio, reaction time, weak areas, relative percentile, and a bunch of other factors, but I didn't care. It just felt good to win once in a while.

I looked around for Seldon once I got out of the avenger but didn't find him. I started home. The high feeling stayed with me until I was almost back to my apartment.

Putting my thumb against the lock, I realized how strongly I wanted Sal to be on the other side of the door when it opened. I felt a bit helpless to think that I still wanted her after the way she had treated me.

The door swung wide to reveal the same old empty room. No Sal.

Sometimes, when we had been together, it seemed that Sal spent ninety-five percent of her time talking about herself or interrupting me and five percent of the time complaining that I never told her anything about myself. She was a remedial listener. But right then I would have traded quite a lot just for that.

That night, for the first time in a long time, I dreamed. Or at least I remembered dreaming when I awoke. I couldn't recall any specific details, but it was unsettling.

The day went downhill from there. This time I was almost expecting it, but the new summons from Arthur still rattled me. The only good thing was that, based on my last check on uptime GS levels, this might be the last time I'd have to endure Arthur.

chapter
SEVEN

I knew that I was in big trouble this time because Arthur didn't make me wait.

Rob waved me right on by without meeting my gaze. I drew a deep breath and walked in. Skipping his usual time-wasting, Arthur came right to the sore point.

"Mike, you're fired. Three weeks' pay will be posted to your account by this afternoon. You will remove your personal possessions from your office by ten hundred hours. That will be all." He looked back down at his desk, indicating that there was no room for discussion.

I had anticipated something like this, but I was still stunned to have it actually happen. Slightly shell-shocked, I half turned to leave before catching myself.

"Now, just a minute." I tried to remain calm. "I'd like to know why." There wasn't much more to lose.

"I will not play your stupid little game. Just get out."

"Arthur, you're *going* to tell me why. You owe me that."

"One last time. You know damn well that it's because of the threat."

"Threat? What are you talking about?"

"Oh, come on."

"Don't stop me if you've heard this already, but I don't have the vaguest idea what you're talking about. I didn't make any threat."

"Just get out. I don't need this irritation."

"*You* don't need this irritation? Who's losing his job here? Who's being judged guilty without a trial or even a hearing? I did not make any threats."

"I suppose that message was accidentally originated by some computer? And that all those personal details were picked out by random selection?"

"I didn't send you any message, threatening, criticizing, or otherwise. Why can't you accept that?" I knew that I wasn't going to win the argument, and I was already aware that nothing I could say would change his mind, but I felt compelled to try.

"I've taken all I am going to. Get out."

"But, Arthur, I—"

"Out!"

I looked at his red face and clenched jaw. His narrowed eyes and slightly hunched frame both added to his body language. I didn't need an interpreter to understand. There wasn't going to be any progress here.

Without another word, I left. It had finally happened.

I waved to Rob to tell him there were no hard feelings and started back to my office, wondering at the calm with which I was taking the situation now. The night that Sal left me had been worse, but being fired was another event that I never had anticipated until recently. The only help for it was the scapescope warning. I had at least been able to brace myself somewhat for the shock.

In a way, the worst was over. I had found out earlier about being fired. Today was just the official notification. But I couldn't convince myself that it was that simple. Sure, I knew before, but to really be living through it was different.

And there were still no clues to what would happen next. In fact, what was to come next could easily be even worse.

Back in my office I took less than a minute to gather up my few possessions. My tiny stack included a small holo of Sal, my personal memory storage attachment for the terminal, and a couple of desk trinkets. I had no intention, however, of leaving the office yet.

This was my last opportunity for at least a while, perhaps forever, to use a scapescope and a terminal that had higher than public-domain access. I meant to take advantage of the chance.

I checked the uptime GS-level awards for my name. I was a no-show, indicating that it was statistically unlikely that I would be swept back under the wing of the government during the next several months. Things just got better and better.

Under my direction the computer checked all uptime criminal identifications against my acquaintance list. No matches, so I must still be alone or in the company of strangers.

I started to go deeper into the data base, but suddenly the "update in progress" sign sprang up on the screen. I tried several related requests on the computer, but it gave me the same message as scapescope. Certain that someone was blocking my access, I started to make other requests.

Several times I received the information that I asked

for, but I kept running into the same block. I continued for over an hour, probing in one place after another until I began to see the pattern.

Each area of data was thoroughly cross-indexed, so I could trace a thread in numerous directions. I could get to the same information by following the threads from various starting points. No matter where I started, I ran into a barrier surrounding a body of data. And each new attempt allowed me to more tightly define the affected statistics.

I didn't like what I saw.

I was staring at the screen, trying to figure out what to explore next, when the text was cleared and replaced with a new message.

"Authorizations are terminated for Michael Cavantalo."

That was it. I could possibly find out the password for one of my shiftmates, but I'd never be able to fool the voice ID system.

The office suddenly felt more confining than before. It had been my daytime refuge for a long time. The message on the screen made things somehow more believable than Arthur's pronouncement. He wasn't much easier to argue with than a computer, but there always existed the small chance that he might take the human prerogative and question the situation, maybe wonder if what was going on were really right.

Not the computer. "I'm only doing my job," it might say.

I picked up my belongings and walked out. I hadn't gone far when I came to a mail chute. Not wanting to go back to my apartment just then, I dropped my stuff in the slot and tapped in my address.

Then a delayed reaction hit me. What about money? Maybe deep down I hadn't believed scapescope. Maybe

I'd thought it would all miraculously work out. But I had only enough funds for perhaps a month or two.

Certain it would be a waste of time, but since there weren't too many choices, I went over to the placement service. At least I could get on the list for a job. Anyway, who knows? Maybe scapescope could be wrong.

The place was fairly quiet when I got there. Most people must have simply phoned in their requests, since looking for a *different* job isn't quite as traumatic as looking for your *only* job. Several wall screens were showing short segments, illustrating jobs available.

As I neared the desk I found reaffirmation of my belief that nothing is ever easy. If I had come in to tell one of the consultants that I was becoming bored with my GS-75 staff position, that person would probably have turned out to be a tired matron or an indifferent gentleman.

Not this time though. Here I was, coming in to explain that I had been fired and was looking for almost anything at all. And the counselor was one of the loveliest young women I had seen in a long while. There's no justice.

To make matters worse, once she found out my predicament, a slight smile reached her lips. "So you would like to be posted on the 'no restrictions' list?" Her gray-green eyes made me uncomfortable.

"That's right."

"That means that you'll take any job that's offered to you. You do understand?" The smile had reached her eyes, and I had the definite feeling of being teased.

"I do have a few restrictions. It needs to be legal." I looked directly into her eyes. "And I don't particularly care for private employers."

A faint flush crept into her cheeks, and she returned to her checklist. Most of the questions were about my job preferences; my job qualifications were already in the employment data base.

When she finished, she asked, "I suppose you realize that it might be a long, long time before you get another job as a futurist?"

"Yes. Until an hour ago, I had access to a scape-scope."

She busied herself again at the terminal. When she finished, she had me confirm with voice ID. As she watched the screen, she frowned slightly. "I'm surprised," she said a moment later. "There aren't any preliminary matches. Usually there're at least a few unqualified positions pending. I guess you picked a tight time to look for work."

"So, what now?"

"You'll be contacted as soon as anything comes in." She was completely businesslike now. "You want messages directed to your home or wristcomp?"

"Both."

I had done all I could. Every job opening that existed was funneled through the placement service. Even the private employers like General Optronics listed their openings, but they accounted for only a small portion of the total. I went home, wondering if sometime soon I would be a complaint handler or a clerk in some out-of-the-way place. Maybe I could watch a status panel to see if any elevators inexplicably halted.

The next several days passed painfully. I opened up both my wristcomp and home phone to all calls, but the only ones that came through were advertising. The fact that my monthly bill would be smaller because of allowing the ad calls didn't cheer me up very much.

I kept to myself, partly because I wanted to be able to respond quickly to a job possibility. Pavlov would have been proud of me. I quickly found my behavior patterns falling into cycles. The chirp of an incoming call would cause a sudden surge of excitement, which was consistently followed by anger and frustration when I realized the call was not a job offer.

I couldn't stand the situation any longer, so I went back to the placement service office to find out what was going wrong. The first thing that went wrong was that the same woman handled my question.

"I'm sorry, but nothing appears to be wrong with the system," she said after making a few inquiries at her terminal. "We're receiving about the average number of new positions, but they seem to be finding better matches with other clients."

"What do all those other people have that I don't? I didn't put any restrictions down."

"Actually, it's what they *don't* have that you do—a record of having been fired. And I do seem to remember that you had some restrictions."

I didn't know what to say, so I left.

I thought about the situation for a few more hours and finally decided to call Seldon. I hadn't talked to him since I was fired, partly because I had wanted to wait until I found another position. The image that came up on my console told me that I had caught him in his office.

"Hello, Mike. I was going to call you. I haven't seen you in a while."

"I apologize. I've been pretty—ah—busy for the past few days. I'd like to get together again soon, but the reason I called is that I need a favor."

"Sure. What is it?"

"I wanted to know if you could submit a personnel request for a friend of mine—in the unskilled category."

"Well, we have a reasonably full crew, but we do

have a little leeway. How soon can he start?''

"ASAP.''

"What special characteristics should I request, so that I get your friend and not someone else?''

"Request that he's familiar with a standard computer terminal and a scapescope.''

"Scapescope? No one on the unskilled— That's you, right?''

"Yes.'' I told him the rest. He seemed almost as angry as I was about the situation. I declined an invitation to get together and told him that I would call him the next day.

In the meantime I decided to check several government offices personally to see if they used the placement service to find new employees.

They all did—and none of them had any complaints about the system.

The news I got from Seldon the next day came as no surprise. The response to his request was that no one on the roster of available people matched his requirements, but that he would be contacted quickly in the event that anyone was found.

I was convinced that no one would be found. Especially not me.

I was also convinced that behind all the mishaps with Arthur, and behind the fact that my job request was being short-circuited, was one person or one agency. And what worried me most was that both the information blockage that I had identified earlier and the job fiasco pointed to the government itself.

chapter
EIGHT

In the same way that I had known when it was too late to argue with Sal, I was convinced that the government was responsible for what was happening to me. Sometimes I had to see one hundred percent of a situation before I could accept it as fact, but more often the first half or two-thirds convinced me. When I leaped to a conclusion, I didn't usually jump the entire distance.

And the same way I knew when I wouldn't like the ending of a piece of music with a sleazy beginning, I knew that I probably wasn't going to care for the ending of any scheme that started out as this one had. There were no clues to suggest why it was happening to me, so I concentrated on finding out who was responsible.

Who in particular, that is. I was sure that someone working for Brother Sammy was doing it, but that was still a large number of people. The search had narrowed during the last session on my work terminal. The information blockage had centered on the enforcer statistics, so I would begin there.

Anyone who had the ability and authorization to tamper with my data files and transmissions could probably inhibit job placement searches in his spare time. If he had any spare time.

There was one person who now had plenty of spare time—me. I decided to use some of it by visiting the Maryland district enforcer office. I still didn't even know what questions to ask, but I went anyway.

An underground shuttle took me most of the way. The staff was so big they had their own building. A map just inside the door showed approximate directions to the headquarters.

One of the nearby slidewalks took me to the elevator. The office was not only high; it also rated an outside wall with windows. Unfortunately they weren't high enough to see over the next building, but it was still interesting to see the sliver of sky above. Idly I wondered who had the prestigious offices at the top-floor corners.

The receptionist was busy when I entered the office, so I occupied myself with the news screen in the lobby. I had completely forgotten about the elections.

Tomorrow was the day. The analysts, helped quite a bit by scapescope, were predicting the winners, the margins, and a fifteen percent response. The nominal turnout meant the issues were fairly clear-cut again.

I glanced back at the receptionist and saw that he was free. I walked over and gave him my ID.

"I'd like to file a complaint." I still had no better idea. He stuck the ID in a slot before asking me a few questions about the particulars. His bored expression almost made me bored with the whole thing, especially since I had no way of knowing whether or not I might learn anything this way.

While he entered my answers, a nearby wall screen displayed a still enlistment ad showing a couple of

young, sharp-looking cadets entering a sleek aircraft
that I vaguely recognized as a Thunderglider. The cap-
tion read, "Prowl Intercept Group," and the line below
it said, "PIGs have wings." It wasn't too clear where
they prowled or what they intercepted.

The receptionist's voice recaptured my attention.
"Just have a seat over there. You'll be called shortly."

I found a place and settled in. "Shortly" turned out
to mean "in something under an hour." Eventually I
was ushered into another office.

The nametag on the desk identified the stocky, graying man behind it as R. C. Tuxworth. I decided not to
endear myself by greeting him with "Hi, R."

He looked up as I entered and, without offering to
shake hands, motioned me to sit. "I see from your complaint," he said, glancing at his desk display, "that you
feel someone else is responsible for your current situation." He squinted as he spoke.

"That's right."

He leaned back in his chair, apparently giving the case
more consideration now that he knew what I looked
like. I sure hoped that didn't matter. His bushy eyebrows bunched slightly as he looked back at his screen.
"This is a grave charge. Do you feel that this might be
just a prank set up by a friend?"

"First of all, I don't have any friends that bad. Second, I don't have any friends who have access to the
power required to handle this. It has to be someone in
the enforcers, but I don't even know anyone in the
force."

"That's simply absurd, Mr. Cavantalo. We do not
manipulate people, we simply enforce the laws. There's
quite a difference."

"You can speak for all the enforcers?"

"Of course not. Each enforcer branch is autonomous. But I am well acquainted with the laws, especially the ones that govern our own operations. Manipulation of law-abiding citizens is not a part of our charter."

"But manipulation of *non*-law-abiding citizens is?"

"Absolutely not. We enforce laws. We do not indulge in entrapment."

"But there's something going on. Who else can change passwords and authorization levels for your sections of the national data base?"

"No one. But it's not at all clear that permissions were changed. You might have made a mistake, or someone may have taken actions that would produce similar symptoms."

"I didn't make a mistake."

"Very well. I'll put in a request to the computer crime section. They should be able to get to it fairly soon."

"How soon might 'fairly soon' be?" I asked mildly.

"I'd guess maybe two or three weeks, depending on their backlog."

"Two or three weeks? Isn't there any way to speed things up?"

"That is speeded up. This time last year their backlog was one to two months." He rose from his chair to signal the end of our conversation.

"But, I—oh, never mind." In the face of my previous experience with the system, there didn't seem to be anything I could say to hasten the process. Frustration began to push back in on me.

Somehow I'd expected that someone with a window office would get instantaneous results. Wrong again. I was ready for anyone to tell me that the tooth fairy was a myth. For all I knew, Tuxworth had been the one responsible for recent events. I just couldn't tell. Things obviously weren't going to get any better soon, so on my way back to my building I called Seldon.

We met later that afternoon to play tennis. We didn't play often. With space at such a premium, the fees were set high in an effort to encourage leisure activities with much smaller area-to-people ratios. In light of my financial condition, Seldon paid. We split sets before running out of energy.

The party next to us had been playing triples, probably in an effort to keep the expense down. I was old-fashioned enough to think that if you couldn't at least afford doubles, you should pick another sport. But it was their money.

We left the courts and found an alcove in a nearby cafeteria.

I was in a quiet mood, so Seldon had to start the conversation. "I made a few more tries to line up a job."

"And?" I was sure I'd have already known if there had been any positive results.

"And no luck. I tried virtually asking for you by name, by specifying four screenfuls of qualifications. It seems that the system doesn't know about you. You want to tell me what happened?"

Little by little I told him portions, and he prompted me for more. He was quiet, too, when he knew as much as I did.

"So, what next?" he asked at length.

"I don't really know. A few muddled ideas come to mind. I'd pigeonhole the guy I saw today in the dumb-but-honest category. I don't think his office has anything to do with this. But he did say that each enforcer section is autonomous. Maybe someone is taking individual initiative."

"What do you think the chances are?"

"Absolutely no idea. But that's all I can think of for now. Even if it pays off, there's still the 'Why me?' question."

"I feel pretty useless. Is there anything I can do to help?"

"Not that I can think of, but thanks, Seldon. The moral support is worth a lot."

We said good-bye and I went back home to take a hot shower. I had just begun to get comfortable when the water suddenly turned scalding hot.

I fell out of the shower, trying to get out of the water's path. I stood up. A cautious glance at the water temperature told me that it was already back down around 40 degrees Celsius, but I turned off the water and dried myself. I was clean enough already, and I didn't need to waste any more water, so I padded down the hallway to my apartment.

I didn't sleep well that night, but the disturbing thing was that instead of worrying about my job, I lay awake for hours wondering where Sal might be. Random fragments of past arguments with her came floating into my thoughts. At least once she had complained that I was taking her for granted.

In a sense I had been. It had seemed to me there were good and bad forms of taking someone for granted. Assuming that a woman's affection for you would always be there no matter how you treated her was a swift road to failure.

But taking a woman for granted—in the sense that, as long as you treated her as well as or better than you would like to be treated, she would treat you accordingly—wasn't entirely bad. It gave a sense of security and belonging that didn't exist if the woman was wildly erratic in her responses to everyday pressures. It didn't mean you could relax and not do your part; it just meant that there existed a bond of mutual trust.

Lying there, I missed that stability almost as much as I missed Sal. In fact, maybe most of the hurt came from the realization that someone close could so easily believe that I would commit a crime. Sal and I hadn't been serious about a long-term relationship, but she could have been more reluctant to believe scapescope.

When I awoke the next morning, I knew what I was going to do that day. But first I needed a name. A couple of minutes at my desk terminal gave it to me, so I filed it in my wristcomp and left.

Soon I was in the enforcer building looking at the same map I had seen yesterday. I quickly found the office I wanted—the political-crime enforcer headquarters. I picked a name and announced myself to the receptionist.

"I'm Ralph Adamson. R. C. Tuxworth sent me over to talk to Mr. Krongard," I said, naming the head of the political-crime force. "It's important that I see him soon." And it was. If anyone in the chain had much time for thought, they might want to find out who Adamson was.

I had the briefest wait in recent history. Probably even if they didn't recognize the name Adamson, they did recognize Tuxworth. A clerk who looked hardly old enough to be out of school led me into an office that was almost as large as Tuxworth's was. The nametag was cut in the same style as Tuxworth's, and it told me that my story hadn't been questioned too much so far. I was presumably facing Noah Krongard himself. He was a large man with features more weathered than I expected in a man with a desk job.

"Mr. Adamson. Have a seat, please. I'm told that Mr. Tuxworth sent you over. I'm surprised that I haven't met you before." There was no questioning inflection at the end of his sentence, but the tone made the intent clear.

I didn't know how long I could keep up the farce.

Krongard had penetrating, intelligent eyes, and I lost some of my optimism. "That's primarily because your department has normally conducted its affairs with efficiency and diligence. I'm on the inspector general team, and usually I'm kept pretty busy oiling the squeaky wheels."

"So, are we squeaking, or is this a social visit?" He leaned back in his chair and rubbed his chin.

"I'm afraid this isn't a social call. It's come to R.C.'s attention that not all of the divisions' regulations are being adhered to strictly."

"Go on." His eyes and voice both tightened fractionally.

"The team has become aware of certain activities that involve a smear campaign and unofficial controls placed on non-enforcer-supervised functions, including the placement service. Does this narrow it down, or do you have so many projects in progress that you don't know which one I'm talking about?"

"You make it sound as though those are the only two choices." Again the question was implied but not inflected.

"They are. There's no question that at least one person is being manipulated."

"And whom might this person be?"

"Michael D. Cavantalo."

"I'm sorry, but you've been given highly inaccurate information. This department runs by the books. We don't indulge in manipulation."

"Oh, but you do. We have documented evidence. Before-and-after transcripts, voice recordings, photographs—"

"That's quite enough, Mr. Cavantalo. Would you please leave?"

"What do you—my name is Adamson. Cavantalo is

the victim that my team is investigating."

"Let's stop the charade, all right? I've never heard of an Adamson, no one calls Bob 'R.C.,' and my aide just verified that Bob didn't send anyone over here today." He motioned to his desk screen.

"Well, how do you know that I'm Cavantalo, if you're not responsible for the tampering?"

"Simple. You were crusading for a Mr. Cavantalo." Simple. But there had been the faintest fraction of a delay before his response.

"I don't accept that. You've been messing around with my reputation, and I want to know why." Somehow I didn't quite say what I meant.

"I have no intention of humoring you, Mr. Cavantalo. I'm a busy man. Would you please show yourself out?"

"No. I've been asked to leave so many offices lately, I'm becoming immune. I want to know what is going on, and I intend to raise the largest stink you've run across in a long time."

"Is that so?"

"Count on it."

He paused to think for a moment, but his manner gave me the impression that he wasn't too impressed. His next words supported that observation. "Mr. Cavantalo, I really don't give a damn about your threat. You probably won't believe me, but, for an entirely different reason, I think we should have a little talk."

He pushed a button and the door slid shut behind me. Then he casually swiveled a small status display so that I could see it. Most of it was evidently devoted to special-purpose functions, but I did recognize the image that filled the graphics area. It was a picture of my face.

"I'd like to explain part of the reason for the following conversation. The likeness of you confirms your identity. You see the word 'clear' on the list on the left?"

I nodded and he continued. "That indicates there are no monitors or recorders present in this room, other than my own. Your wristcomp record and transmit functions are currently inhibited. You don't even have any implants, unless they're organic. Therefore, whatever is said here is just between us."

He leaned forward and put his hands on the desk. "I want this to be very clear. You will have as much trouble proving what will go on in here as you will trying to prove that you have been manipulated."

Krongard leaned back in his chair. "Because you have been."

chapter
NINE

"You're admitting that you've been manipulating me? Just like that?" I could hardly believe the acknowledgment had come so easily. The good news was that I wasn't a paranoid. I'd just heard the bad news.

"Yes," Krongard said. "There's no longer any reason to conceal the fact. Now that you've done enough checking to arrive here, it's a bit bothersome to continue. This is just somewhat premature."

"Does that mean that you'll reinstate me?" His tone of voice implied no encouragement, but I had to ask.

"Hardly. It simply means that a change in plans may be required."

"You're damn right a change will be required. What's going on?"

Krongard hesitated before replying. "Quite simply, we need a favor."

"You mean this whole fiasco was designed to get me to fix you up with a date?"

"Very cute, Mr. Cavantalo. No, the favor is more complicated than that. And, as is probably obvious from recent events, it may not be something you've been eagerly waiting to do.''

"And it's probably obvious to you from recent events that even a small favor would be an uphill struggle." I would have walked out right then, but I couldn't leave without knowing what it was all about.

"Let me be very clear on this point. We require your assistance. I had hoped to instill in you a receptive mood, but we have not exhausted our repertoire of methods to obtain your cooperation.''

"Well, how about if you tell me exactly what you want, and I'll decide if it appeals to me?''

"Very well. Briefly, we want you to infiltrate a group of people who are, in all likelihood, working on a project that may well be a threat to the government and, therefore, to all citizens.''

"Are you joking?''

"I'm absolutely serious. I don't take my work lightly.''

"But I don't have any spying abilities. I'm just an average guy.''

"Wrong. You have a couple of important qualifications that I will get to shortly.''

"But—''

"Mr. Cavantalo, just let me explain the situation without all the interruptions. It will go a lot faster.''

I just nodded.

"First of all, location. You might be wondering where this group is, and why we can't simply arrest the members. The answer is that they have picked a location that is inaccessible to us. As long as we assume that there will be no deaths, that is. We could either destroy the installation or take it by force, but either way all or most of the group would be killed. And besides the fact that we have strict guidelines prohibiting unnecessary killing, there probably are some extremely valuable people there."

He paused while he punched a few keys on his console to bring up a picture on the wall screen. It showed a fairly typical mountain scene with a few ragged peaks almost submerged in the buildings that clustered about the foothills.

"This is a photo of the Colorado Rockies, on the fringe of the Pueblo-Springs metro area. How is your history, Mr. Cavantalo? Your military history."

"Weak."

"The peak near center screen is Cheyenne Mountain. That's the site of one of three or four abandoned WATCH installations."

"WATCH?"

"Western Alliance Tactical Command Headquarters. There was another in the Mojave Region, installed when it was still a desert. There was at least one other elsewhere. This is one of the oldest. It's been around so long that it was originally used by a joint command of the United States and Canada."

"Where is it? I can't see anything on the screen."

He punched a few more keys and the image started to zoom. The area of interest was probably just above the edge of the line of buildings, because that was the center of zoom. After a few more seconds a couple of old, boxy buildings grew large enough to be visible.

"Those buildings sure don't look all that impregnable."

"They aren't." He shifted the view slightly to the right, but the only thing I saw was a tunnel entrance.

"It's on the other side of the mountain?"

"No, it's inside."

"You're joking."

"No, I'm not. The complex is buried about half a

klick into the mountain. It was originally constructed back in the mid-nineteen hundreds, when fortification was more important than concealment. It was continually upgraded until it was finally decommissioned sometime aorund 2070. The expense of taking care of it or turning it into a museum didn't justify keeping it, so they finally sold the complex for salvage.''

"Mr. Krongard, I think you've got the wrong guy. I don't think I could even find the doorbell."

"Spare me, please. No one is going into that complex uninvited. Besides the fact that they've got doors and locks designed to withstand nearby atomic blasts, they've got antipersonnel defenses that include lasers and neuron paralyzers. And there's no way to cut them off. They've got an old fusion generator and a stockpile of supplies. They can communicate with people on the outside with short-blast neutrino transmitters that are virtually untraceable. It's really quite a setup."

"How is it that you know so much about them?"

"We've had, ah—contact with a resident in there previously."

"So why didn't you get him to take care of things for you?"

"Let's just say that we haven't heard from him recently."

"Swell. My God, Krongard, you sure don't do anything by halves. But you picked the wrong guy this time. I'm no secret-agent type. I can't even hold two aces with a straight face. I've got no qualifications or interest, ignoring the business of coercion. I suggest you throw me back and go looking for a bigger fish."

"You're quite wrong about qualifications." Krongard was calm. "Did you hear that Celeste Newbury was recently reported missing?"

"So?"

"So, we feel reasonably certain that she is with the group, either as an accomplice or under duress."

"Like I said. So?"

"We think they're working on scapescope modifications, perhaps to extend the viewing time well past the six-month limitation—maybe even a year." He said it like he might have said that they were planning to kill every man, woman, and child on Earth.

"Maybe we'd make better progress if you'd just explain your logic as we go along. I fail to see why that would be so terrible. We could take advantage of benefits even farther uptime. So what?"

"But they are working for their own purposes, not the government's. All the scapescopes in existence are controlled by the government, for the protection of the public. Who knows what advantage the ability to see farther uptime would give some dissident group? They could maneuver events that the government can't even see yet."

I wasn't convinced. "But even if they could develop a longer range, which I don't really see as any big threat, why involve me? I've used scapescopes, maybe I could even troubleshoot portions of the circuits, but I'm not a specialist on their overall design."

"I know that. It's just a bonus that you're familiar with them. There's a much better reason why you were picked for this job."

"What's that?"

"You already know one of the group members quite well. She's your sister. That qualification alone should get you inside."

"What? Pat's in that group?"

"Yes. That is one of the few facts of which we are positive."

"You're crazy. Pat's not some nutty building-bomber. Either she's got no part of that bunch, or they're not at all what you think they are. She wouldn't have anything to do with a radical organization. It's that simple.''

"I assure you, Mr. Cavantalo, she is a member of that group, and they are working on their own projects. And they are making genuine efforts to keep their work secret. They're not going to let just anybody in.''

"I suppose that Arthur Springer has been working for you all this time?'' I asked.

"Hardly. A few well-placed rumors were enough to influence the situation. I had hoped that you'd be unaware of my participation.''

"Well, you can just find yourself another body. I can't believe this. You've dumped on me, destroyed my job, blocked my attempts to get another one, and now you want me to infiltrate some undoubtedly innocent group and betray my sister. Shove it.''

"I realize that this conversation is somewhat premature. We had intended to wait until you were more tractable. And we can afford to wait a little while longer.''

"I've heard all I care to listen to. You're going to have a very long wait, Mr. Krongard. And I'm going to be a busy little boy explaining to a few other government departments about your extracurricular activities and your interferiority complex. Good-bye.'' I was almost feeling good about leaving someone's office without being ordered to, but the mood faded abruptly.

"Mr. Cavantalo,'' he said, rising from his chair. "Make absolutely no mistake about this. You won't be able to convince *one* person about what's been going on. The few people with any actual knowledge are extremely good at their jobs and are just as patriotic as I am. And one more thing. If you're saying anything to yourself like, 'at least things can't get any worse,' don't listen. Because that little voice is dead wrong.''

The door slid open, and as I strode out he added, "I'll be seeing you, Mr. Cavantalo." The confidence in his voice shook me more than his earlier speech.

It was as though he had stolen some of my confidence to bolster his. I was angry, but it was still all too new to absorb totally. My recent mishaps couldn't have been mistakes or coincidences. Several pointers led to Krongard's office. But to have him actually admit it totally unsettled me.

In terms of clashing clichés, my ship finally came in and there I was, up a creek without an oar.

Fortunately shuttles didn't require oars, so I was able to make my way back to my own building. The trip gave me more time for the reality of the situation to sink in. I wandered about for several hours, not paying much attention to where I was going, but noticing the familiar blue-and-gold enforcer uniform several more times than seemed reasonable.

Now I knew that the observation must simply be one of Krongard's forms of harassment. That, too, annoyed me. At that moment I truly envied Krongard's power. He was running a floodlamp compared to my nightlight.

And my nightlight was flickering.

In retrospect it seemed like a silly time to go shopping, but buying something usually improved my spirits when they were low. I couldn't afford much, considering the status of my account, but I went looking anyway.

After window-shopping for a while, I found a shop that offered art prints. A small black-and-white mountain scene caught my eye, and after a brief struggle with my conscience, I decided to buy it.

As long as I had decided to buy one, I might as well have picked an expensive mural, because when the clerk rang up the sale, the terminal flashed a message I had never seen before: OUT OF FUNDS.

"There's got to be a mistake," I started. "I know that —oh, no." It suddenly occurred to me that whatever this was, it was not a mistake. *Damn Krongard.*

In a rage I left the shop and wandered around still more. So he had drained what little I had left in my account. Or at least, he was prohibiting me from spending on luxuries. To further test the theory, I tried to buy dinner, emphasis on "tried."

No good. I had absolutely zero funds. And if I transferred some in, they would probably vanish also.

In more ways than one it was a good time to go see Seldon.

It was good timing also. I found him just as he was leaving work. Fifteen minutes later we were eating dinner in a nearby cafeteria, courtesy of Seldon's account. Between bites I recounted the day's events, trying to eat slowly despite the tension.

Seldon asked only a few questions as I related the story. When I was finished, he said, "This guy Krongard really sounds like a sweetheart. What do you plan to do?" I could see in his eyes that he shared my pain.

"First of all, I probably won't be eating my meals alone. I'd be surprised if my account can retain any funds."

As an experiment we both tapped a few keys on our wristcomps and transferred a small sum from his account into mine. I watched the account-balance display. It took only a couple of seconds before it flashed back to zero.

"I don't know for sure what they're doing, but I bet that, as a minimum, my account probably now has a swarm of standing orders for stuff that I don't know or care about."

"What next?" he asked.

"Well, I'm sure as hell not going to betray my sister. I think this whole thing is going to turn into a waiting game. If I can just outlast them, either the project will end or they'll realize their coercion isn't going to work. If I can get a loan from you for buying food, I should be able to get by."

"Of course. You should already know that." His smile made the statement emphatic.

"They probably can't kick me out of my apartment unless I'm declared dead, but I don't think they're going to try anything that could actually be disproved or traced to them. That's a little help."

"Let me do some checking, Mike. There's probably a way for me to pay for some books and music on my account and have them routed to your apartment."

"Thanks. That would make the wait a lot easier."

We parted after making arrangements for meeting at breakfast. I felt like relaxing with some quiet, so I went back to my apartment.

It was peaceful there for over an hour, but then Krongard's cronies pulled one more stunt.

One minute the apartment was light; the next it was dark.

The bastards had cut my power. And power was the lifeblood of that entire room. Without power nothing worked. The lights, heating, cooling, communications, computer, all dead.

To some people it might have seemed like complaining that an assassin who shot me had also made a hole in my shirt, but what bothered me even more about the lack of power was that it was also necessary for books and music. Krongard must have spent a long time with my personal file.

chapter
TEN

I was now powerless, in both senses.

Damn Krongard anyway. If I had been maintaining a list of his character traits, I would put "thorough" much higher than it had been before. Not only had he managed to get the power to my apartment cut off; he had somehow disabled the local battery. I had never experienced even a temporary blackout, since the batteries normally kicked in if the external voltage dropped too low.

Briefly I considered going out, but decided against it in favor of going to sleep. I wasn't that tired, but I felt worn down by the struggle. The glow of my wristcomp told me that Krongard hadn't found a way to disable it, *yet*.

I didn't even take off my clothes. I just grappled around until I found the bed, folded it down, and climbed in. Knowing that my desk computer would be inoperative, I set my wristcomp for an 0800 wakeup.

I needn't have bothered. By 0300 I was wide-awake, rasping stale air in a sweltering 35-degree-Celsius heat.

I stumbled toward the door, swearing at my newly stubbed toe and my lack of foresight. I should have realized what would happen without air-conditioning and filtering.

Panic hit me momentarily as the door failed to slide open, but then I remembered the manual override. I fumbled at the panel covering it and turned the wheel inside. Slowly a vertical gap widened, opening into the hallway. As soon as it was wide enough to squeeze through I did so, drawing deep breaths of cool, fresh air.

I stood there in the now deserted hall, squinting in the light. My perspiration evaporated rapidly in the dry air, and the chill felt good at first.

That was about the only thing that felt good, however. No job, no income, no apartment, no solution.

Seldon's help was now more necessary than ever, but there was no point in waking him. I sent him a low-priority message so he would see it in the morning but it wouldn't wake him. For the time being, the cafeteria would have a comfortable place to sit.

I rubbed the sleep out of my eyes as the elevator carried me down ten levels. But it stopped without opening its doors. I'd been here before. This time I settled down to wait, almost too tired to be even angrier.

The elevator wasn't to be stuck for hours this time, though. Shortly after the halt Krongard's low, teasing voice came over the speaker.

"I think it's time we stopped playing games, Mr. Cavantalo. You've got firsthand knowledge of my capabilities. Meet me in my office at 0900 and be prepared to cooperate, or we start on Seldon Lanyard." I had firsthand knowledge all right. Straight from the horse's ass.

The speaker went dead. I didn't say a word. The communication smelled thoroughly one-way. A moment later the elevator resumed its journey, soon depositing me on the right level.

I rested my head on a cafeteria table, making several resolutions as I sat. Krongard probably wouldn't be in until 0900, but I'd be there waiting for him. I could sleep there just as easily as here.

I started on my way, feeling like a person who asked a firm one hundred dollars for a widget and then snapped up the first offer of twenty-five. Fortunately shuttles and slidewalks were free and still on automatic. I keyed in my destination and settled back. The shuttle trip to Krongard's building went more slowly than the last time. Only the gentle *whoosh* of wind streaming over the outer surface of the shuttle disrupted the quiet stillness. There were a few people up and around, but most everyone must have been asleep or working the midshift.

The shuttle dropped me off at Krongard's building. The remainder of the trip was jerky because each new slidewalk I came to was stopped until I stepped onto it. When I reached his office, I stretched out in the lobby and tried to sleep. I couldn't, naturally, but I was able to relax slightly and rest my eyes. Time crept until finally distant sounds of conversation signaled the start of the dayshift. Pulling myself into one of the chairs, I tried to look like an early riser casually waiting for Krongard.

I couldn't tell if they were fooled or not. Then again, what did it matter? Krongard wasn't the first to arrive, but he was close.

I don't think he even broke his stride. As he saw me a slight, smug smile formed on his lips, and he said, "Good morning, Mr. Cavantalo. I trust you slept well. Come on in, won't you?"

One urge to kill, hold the rape and pillage. I walked in without talking.

Once his door slid shut, I began to tell him what I thought, my temper held barely in check. "You really have a way of eliminating options, you slimy son of a bitch." I tried to rant and rave long enough to convince him that I was going to cooperate, and finally paused to catch my breath. "What do you want done?"

"Easy, Mr. Cavantalo. Just relax. You may not like the methods we employ, but the goal is certainly a valid and necessary one."

"You can take the means and shove them up the justified end."

"The means are different for each individual. For a person with an acutely developed sense of patriotism, a straightforward request is ordinarily enough enticement. Your profile was not such a simple case." He must have meant that I wasn't a mindless drone.

"Let's get on with it."

"Very well. We need to discuss two topics. The first is the location. The WATCH site, that is. I think it will be safer for you to know nothing about the site that couldn't be learned from the unclassified data base. If you know any more than that, it will be only a matter of time before you make a slip that demonstrates that you have been briefed."

"That sounds reasonable."

"Mr. Cavantalo, I'm not asking for your approval. I'm explaining my rationale so you don't feel the urge to ask me a lot of stupid questions that you don't really need answered right now."

I shut up.

"Now, if I may continue. Here's the picture from the outside."

On the screen he displayed another view of the tunnel entrance he had shown me earlier.

"That's the main entrance, the north portal," he said. "The tunnel joins this entrance with the south portal, which is used for service. The complex itself is reached via several doors set parallel with the tunnel, which curves. That way the shock waves from a nearby detonation simply travel along the tunnel.''

"They actually expected this place to withstand a nearby hit?"

"Yes. And with good reason." He punched another button and a picture of a large metal door came up on the screen. "This is the main entrance. The door may not look all that impressive to you. That is, until you know it's over twice as tall as you are, and it masses about twenty-three thousand kilos."

"I'm impressed. I'm impressed."

"That's good, because if you weren't, I'd point out the fact that forty-five meters behind this door there's another one just like it. As I mentioned last time, they also have several types of defenses and counter-offenses. When the facility was decommissioned, those systems were rendered inoperative, but the group restored some of the originals and added a few of their own. You shouldn't have to worry about those systems, though. If they don't want you in, you won't get in."

"That's fine with me."

"The size of those doors should give you an idea of the magnitude of the complex. They didn't skimp when they were scooping out granite to make the central chamber. It covers more than four acres."

"Wouldn't the roof give way?"

"It's not one huge cavern. They left the rock in place here and there, between buildings." With those words he flashed another view on the screen. "That's one of the oldest buildings. Notice the big supports that look like large springs?"

"Yes."

"They *are* springs—to damp out shock waves from nearby explosions or tremors. I think by now you have a feel for the size of the installation.''

"That's safe to say," I replied.

"Good. That brings us to the second topic. Which is, what we expect of you. Briefly, we want you to get access to the complex and bring the project to a halt or get us in. Clear enough?"

"Now wait a minute here. What exactly do you mean by 'bring it to a halt'?" I hoped that my complaining sounded legitimate. He might get even more unpleasant if he knew I had absolutely no intention of following his instructions. At least as far as hurting Pat or the project was concerned. I did intend to go through the motions. But I'd make up my own mind about the project.

"Easy, Mr. Cavantalo. No one needs to get hurt." He went on to explain what I would have to do. When he finished, he told me what arrangements would be necessary for the trip to Colorado. Part of my cover turned out to be that my name was added to the list of known political criminals. No wonder none of my efforts had been able to reveal what the cause would be.

"One more thing," he continued. "When this is all finished satisfactorily, you'll be reinstated and there will be a five-year salary bonus deposited in your account, along with your previous balance."

I almost lost my composure then. Had it not been for the need to convince him that I was going along with this stupid scheme, I would have told him what he could do with his reward right then. And I didn't point out that the reinstatement was necessary only because of him. "Fair enough," I said, when my throat loosened. "When does this all start? Do I go out and hijack a plane?"

"Don't be ridiculous. In some ways this group is relatively naive. All indications are that they don't have privileged links into the main systems. We can provide you transportation most of the way. Be at the roof port of your building at 1700. Any other questions?"

"Yes. What are my restrictions between now and then?"

"Use your own judgment—with one exception. Don't mention this to any of your friends, including Mr. Lanyard."

"Not even that I'm leaving for a while?"

"That much is acceptable, but there must be no mention of your plans."

"All right. Is that all?" I had to get busy making preparations.

"Yes. You won't forget those destination codes for messages?"

"No." I left Krongard's office, still in a foul mood, but now I had the glimmerings of a few ideas coalescing in the back of my mind.

Back at my apartment I had to use the manual override again. The power was still off. The light from the hall gave me enough visibility to grab the personal effects that meant the most to me.

In the corridor I called Seldon on my wristcomp.

"Seldon, can you get off work for a while? I'm taking a trip, so I wanted to leave some of my belongings with you and say good-bye."

He must have caught the tone in my voice, because he didn't hesitate a fraction or ask why. "Sure. Meet you at my place?"

"Thanks."

I beat him there by only a few minutes. "Are you doing okay?" he asked when he saw me.

"Yes. An unexpected trip just came up. Can I impose on you to keep these for me?" I held up my bag.

"Of course. You should know that. Come on in."

Once the door was shut, I said, "I can't tell you anything about the trip, but it looks like I'll be gone for at least a few weeks." As I talked, I winked and put my finger to my lips. The odds that I was still carrying an audio bug were immense, but I felt confident that there was no video surveillance.

A tiny smile replaced Seldon's frown.

"Well, all right, if you say so. Is there anything you need?" he asked.

"Yes. Can I use your desk terminal for a few minutes? I want to get a few maps printed out for the trip."

"Help yourself. I've got a few minutes of makework to finish up as long as I'm home."

I held up an okay sign, knowing that Seldon knew exactly what I had in mind. Krongard might have an idea, also, but he couldn't know for sure.

I went over to his terminal and switched it off-line to disconnect it from the outside net. Quickly I typed in, I SAW KRONGARD AGAIN. I'M GOING TO INFILTRATE.

I looked over my shoulder and found Seldon right behind me. I continued. THEY WANT THE PROJECT HALTED.

Seldon nudged me over and typed, AT WHAT COST?

HE SAYS NO DEATH BUT NOT SURE I TRUST.

We went on for another five or six minutes. Before we stopped, we set up the structure of a com link that Krongard wouldn't be able to break very easily, and we picked coded identifications for each of us to use with a blind-drop com center. I didn't know if I would need any help from Seldon, or even if he would be able to help, but knowing that I could contact a friend on the outside if I needed to made me feel better.

I just hoped that the mountain complex was tied directly into the net. If I had to make a trip into town to use a terminal, it wouldn't be a lot of help.

"Thanks, Seldon. Take care of yourself," I said after we completed the arrangements.

"Right. And have a nice trip." I knew what he meant.

I could have stayed the rest of the afternoon, but it seemed best not to attract any more attention to Seldon than I already had. I roamed the corridors for a few hours, waiting for 1700 to roll around.

I would rather have waited for an audit. The hours wouldn't pass quickly enough. By 1630 I was at the roof port, hoping that someone would land early.

At least the view was nice. The sun broke through the clouds only occasionally, so I didn't have to worry about a burn. The horizon was far enough into the distance that the buildings turned blue and blurry. At sporadic intervals small subsonic craft came close enough to my building for me to hear the Doppler effect at the closest approach.

Finally at 1655 a small dual-rotor copter landed. The pilot waved me inside.

"Hop in, Mr. Cavantalo," he called over the *whup-whup-whup*. He gave off a faint air of boredom as I climbed up, but as he went over the instruments he struck me as a relaxed, thorough, and competent guy. Of course, I couldn't tell if he was even going to fly the craft himself or let navnet do it, but he put on a good show.

A short flight took us maybe thirty kilometers over building after building, the regularity broken only twice by natural features of the land. We landed at Wright airport.

After a brief wait I boarded a much larger craft, probably a Sabersonic. It was a commercial flight, so there was lots of company. Feeling fairly antisocial, I looked out the window a lot.

Casually I wondered why, on such a modern, sophisticated craft, the interior lights flickered. The view grew boring once we were high enough that the spaces between buildings became invisible, so I shut my eyes and tried to relax.

We landed near central Colorado before the light faded. As we were coming in I got a good view of the Rockies, several kilometers west of Stapleton Central. A narrow, dark strip marked the gap between the snow above and buildings below.

I spent the night in temporary quarters near the airport. The next morning I took a shuttle from what the locals referred to as Denver, south to the Pueblo-Springs section of the Rockies Beltway. All along the trip were buildings that seemed to be trying to force the mountains west to the coast. Besides the mountains themselves, about the only difference I noticed was that there was a much higher percentage of solar collectors here than in the Maryland area.

I switched shuttles at the proper intersection, and soon the new shuttle began to climb. My ears popped several times before I reached the end of the line. The rental car lot was conveniently close.

I was glad to avoid walking the balance of the journey. Just strolling to the car lot partially winded me at that altitude.

The cars were mostly all-terrain vehicles with oversize tires. I'd had little opportunity to drive, and I felt awkward pulling out of the lot. Fortunately there was almost no other traffic.

After less than half a kilometer I left the buildings behind me. I found an ancient, weatherbeaten, potholed road right where Krongard had said I would. It meandered upward for over a kilometer before it took a hairpin turn to the left and climbed more steeply.

The road decreased its climb and started another turn to the left when I saw the tunnel entrance. I continued on the road for another fifty meters and found a leveled area that had to be an old parking lot with a portion marked off for copters. The decaying pavement had huge cracks through which hardy grass thrived.

I left the car with its panels pointing south and set on sun-track so it would get a full charge. I typed in a password that it would require before permitting any further use and left it. I hoped that I would be able to use it again.

A decrepit chain-link fence barred my way. Certain that any place with defenses like Krongard had described would have as much use for an electrified fence as they would for a welcome mat, I was still hesitant to touch it before I knew for sure. Then I noticed that the bottom of the fence was partially covered with dirt, increasing the odds against electrification.

On the strength of that observation, I flicked my fingertips so they brushed briefly against a couple of links. Nothing. Moments later I was on the other side. Evidently the fence had been put there just to discourage the public.

The builders may not have put much emphasis on exterior fortifications, but apparently they did at least want to know what was happening on the outside. There were several video cameras along the way.

One of them tracked me as I walked the rest of the way to the tunnel entrance. That was fine with me. I didn't want to be too big of a surprise.

No one challenged me as I started into the tunnel. It was big, maybe ten meters high. Large enough to drive two wide vehicles side-by-side. The thought of traffic moved me to use the sidewalk on the right side of the tunnel.

The only light was from the entrance behind me, and as I walked it grew dimmer. I had seen overhead lamps at regular intervals, but I gathered that either they were no longer functional or the crew inside had deliberately turned them off to discourage nonresidents.

The tunnel ran straight into the mountain. A forceful breeze came steadily at me, and the gloom deepened with each step. I thought I could detect a faint rise, but I couldn't be sure. A rise would have made sense, though. It would have been pretty bad planning to design a place this expensive if it flooded during the first heavy rain.

My line of thought was roughly interrupted when I ran painfully into a very unyielding obstacle. After cursing and rubbing my nose and chin, I felt around and satisfied myself that what I had run into was not the end of the line, but just a large metal box mounted on the wall. I couldn't tell anything about its function.

The experience convinced me that I might as well walk on the road after all. I continued, occasionally bumping my right foot on the curb so I could keep to the side of the tunnel. I hadn't gone much farther when I started hitting the curb more frequently than before. That must mean I had finally reached the leftward bend.

And that meant the blast doors were not too far ahead.

After another minute or so I spotted a light. A red glow that first appeared to be on the left wall soon moved to the right wall as I completed the turn. It seemed to be about where the door should be.

It was. The door was bigger than its picture had implied. And, not surprisingly, it was shut.

In the reddish glow I spotted what looked like a speaker grille. Maybe it also concealed a microphone.

"Hello, inside," I called.

"No need to shout. I can hear you fine," came an anonymous, bored voice.

"Let me in."

"Sorry. This installation is off-limits. It's time you were leaving." The voice was masculine with a touch of a rasp.

"I don't intend to. I'd like to come inside."

"Mister, it would be extremely unwise for you to stick around. We have several deterrents. And I'm going to turn on one of the mild ones in thirty seconds."

"No, wait! I'm Mike Cavantalo. Does that name mean anything to you?"

There was a pause.

"Yes and no," the voice said.

"I assume you mean that 'Cavantalo' means something to you and 'Mike' doesn't. I'm Pat's brother."

"I didn't—"

"Well, check it out."

"Hold on."

I heard some clattering as he apparently picked up a phone. I caught snatches of his side of another conversation. ". . . Avon lady out front . . . her brother . . . wants in."

The conversation grew even softer then. After a couple of minutes the voice came back.

"Stand back from the door," it said.

Not knowing how fast the door would move, I backed up quickly. It turned out that I had been overly cautious. I heard a dull clank from deep within the metal, and a pulsing sound started as the door began to swing open. White light filtered through a crack on the right, and soon I began to see more outlines of my surroundings.

It took almost half a minute for the door to swivel all the way to the left. The door looked appreciably more vulnerable from the inside. The outside had been basically a plane, but this side was strewn with hydraulic lines and assorted paraphernalia.

"Come on in," the voice directed when the sounds died out.

Not completely trusting and not absolutely sure that the door *had* to move that slowly, I hurried through and found myself in a cavity between the two doors. The inner one was closed. I felt as though I were in the airlock of a ship built for aliens who were as large as tanks.

The pulsating sound resumed, and the huge door started to pivot closed behind me. It moved just as slowly as before, but as it reached the end of its travel it slammed shut with a disturbing, deep, resounding boom.

"Damn," said the voice.

I was waiting for the inner door to open when the voice said, "Okay, now strip."

"I beg your pardon."

"You heard me, mister. We're very particular about what gets brought in here. If you've got any weapons with you, you're not coming through the door."

"Why the hell wait until now to tell me? Why not tell me all the way outside?"

"This way gives us a lot more leverage, don't you think? On with it—or rather, off with it." I could almost hear his smug grin.

There didn't seem to be any other options. After I stripped, he directed me to put my clothes in a box in the corner and then walk through a scanner at the side of the room. A few minutes later he was apparently satisfied that I didn't have any weapons serious enough for them to worry about. I put my clothes back on, wondering what would happen next.

The pulsing noise resumed, and this time the inner door started to open. By now I was fairly sure that it was moving as fast as it ever did, but when it was fully open I still hurried through. The door was probably a meter thick, and I had absolutely no desire for any practical jokes.

I was about to continue into the tunnel when the voice stopped me.

"Wait! Stop right where you are. There's a laser barrier ten meters into the tunnel.'' This time the voice lacked the metallic intercom distortion.

I looked for the source of the voice and discovered that its owner was in a cubicle directly to my right.

''So what do you want me to do?'' I asked.

''Just sit tight for a few minutes. Pat's on her way.''

Only the top half of his body was visible through the glass, but, unless he was shaped like a bowling pin, he was one of the thinnest people I had seen. He sported a light beard. His jaws moved periodically as he apparently chewed gum.

I waited, looking at the view. The tunnel floor seemed to be an old asphalt material, complete with cracks and potholes. The tunnel itself continued at least as far as the gentle bend less than a hundred meters ahead. Large metal arcs with inset doors on both sides of the tunnel implied branches to other tunnels.

The walls and ceiling were an uneven mixture. Portions appeared to be patched with plasteel. The balance was covered with a metal mesh with small triangles sprinkled around. If the purpose of the mesh was to keep small rocks from falling from the roof, it was doing its job well. In several places it sagged under the weight of small piles of broken rocks.

My inspection was terminated by the sounds of footsteps, apparently coming from around the curve. Another fifteen seconds passed before I saw two figures. One of them I recognized instantly. Even in silhouette Pat's figure and bearing were unmistakable.

''Hi,'' I called.

''Hi,'' she called back, her tone of voice saying, ''So it really is you. What are you doing here?''

chapter
ELEVEN

So Pat really was in the complex. Until then, I
hadn't entirely believed Krongard. I waited to speak until she came closer.

"You sure are a hard person to get an appointment
with," I said.

"That was the whole idea, as I'm sure you know."
The vexation that crept along with her words surprised
me. "What are you doing here?"

"Such a warm greeting. I thought you'd be glad to see
me."

"You know I am. But we've made a great deal of effort to keep a low profile."

"Okay, okay. I'll tell all. But can't we go somewhere
more comfortable?"

In answer she looked at her black-eyed companion,
who made the guard seem almost fat in comparison. He
thought for a moment before he said to the guard,
"Right, Merle. Shut 'em down."

To me he said, "Come ahead."

I stepped past the danger area and joined them. Pat

hooked her arm in mine to let me know that she wasn't totally angry to see me.

"Mike, Don," she said.

We shook hands, and the three of us started back up the tunnel. Somehow the first-name basis didn't comfort me as it normally would have. It was probably better for me not to know last names.

Don's thin-fingered handshake had implied a quiet strength that seemed to spring from a calm self-confidence rather than an extroverted urge to impress. Instinctively I felt that he either led the group making their residence there or was in an influential position. And a group that Pat had joined certainly wouldn't determine influence by family ties or the right school.

Neither of them chose to resume the conversation, so I kept quiet as we walked. Partway through the bend in the main tunnel a partition blocked the opening and forced us to use a small doorway through it. On the other side stood one of the buildings from the pictures that I had seen during my visit to Krongard's office.

It looked like a fairly ordinary windowless building, squeezed into a cave. It should have been a three-story building, but I didn't really get a calibration on it until we were almost at the door and I saw one of the shock-absorbing springs in relation to my height. The roof of the building appeared almost to meet the top of the tunnel, with a few meters to spare.

The air carried a faint odor of things mechanical and oily, and a slight rumble of distant equipment. A few steps took us up to the level of the first floor. The corridor turned right, but no door blocked our way.

"Let's just stop in here," Don said, indicating a door at the end of a short corridor.

The room was evidently a briefing room, with a couple dozen rows of cushioned movie seats, a wall screen at the front, and a glass booth in the rear. Don pointed to the back row, and we sat.

"Your presence here suggests several questions," he said.

The following silence turned the quiet statement into a question. His black eyes were piercing, making it hard to look away from his gaze. I started to talk, wondering how convincing a liar I could be.

"You two seem awfully serious. Have I done anything wrong?" I asked.

"No, Mike," Pat said. "Like I said before, we went to a lot of trouble to get our privacy. We'd just like to know how you found us and why you're here."

I looked at her again before I spoke. If anything, she seemed more utilitarian than before. She wore a plain T-shirt and shorts and little or no makeup. She was serious, but a faint glow showed through. I couldn't tell whether it was because she was glad to see me or she was doing things that gave her more sense of accomplishment than before.

"I guess that 'why' goes before 'how.' The 'why' is pretty simple. I'd like an out-of-the-way place to rest and recuperate for a while. I got on the political criminal list by accident, and I figure that if I can outwait them, they'll get their facts straight. I'd rather they ask questions first and use the 'vegematic' later."

I went on to explain how a woman I had supposedly been involved with had been participating in an effort to influence the outcome of a skirmish down in Brazil. By virtue of seeing her several particular times that turned out to be meeting times, my name had been added to the list.

Also some troubles with a jerk of a boss had caused him to give me a bad recommendation when I needed a good one. My hopes were that once the more legitimate members of the group had been rounded up, their combined responses would satisfy the authorities that I really had not been involved. And I had left a message behind me to that effect.

Neither one appeared to be ready to hand over the key to the city, but neither one openly disputed my tale.

"How is it that you found our location?" Don asked.

"That was the hard part. Before all this came up, I started playing around with scapescope, trying to see if I could find out anything about Pat."

Pat's eyes seemed to narrow slightly at the mention of scapescope, but I couldn't be positive.

"I know you wanted to have your privacy, but I was really curious about you—where you were, what you were doing. At any rate, I set up a search on your activities. And your links with any other people. And something turned up."

This was the weakest part of the story that Krongard had given me, but I hadn't been able to come up with anything more convincing.

"Several months uptime, your name gets linked with the name 'Donald Ottowa.' "

Pat's companion nodded slightly in recognition.

"And," I continued, "a couple of years back, that same name showed up in a public request list. It seems that you were trying to acquire the salvage rights to this complex. There you have it."

They were both silent for a moment before Don spoke.

"And here you are. We're not really set up for visitors, but I think that we might be able to let you stay for a short while." He rose, and Pat did too. "Unfortunately you've caught us at a very busy time, but if you'll wait here for a few minutes, we'll find someone here who can show you around. Pat and I need to get back to our work, but we can talk more tonight.''

I couldn't read his expression or his tone of voice. It could be anything from belief to contempt. I think that he wanted it to seem like belief. I looked back at Pat, but she was on her way out.

"Let's talk more tonight, Mike," she said as she turned back for a moment. "It's good to see you again."

They left the door ajar behind them. I sat for several minutes, wondering how much they had believed. I hadn't lied to Pat since we were young enough to fight about who had eaten the last of the cookies.

My wait ended with the approaching sound of soft footsteps in the hall. The door opened farther and a young, dusty-blond woman came in.

"Michael Cavantalo? Don asked me to give you a tour." Her contralto voice suited her appearance nicely.

Her manner was calm and seemed to convey a slight curiosity. As she came closer I could see the small motions her eyes made as she surveyed me. A strong impression of intelligence came with the brief examination.

"My name is Mike. And I'm all set."

"I'm Lisa Ryan," she said before she turned for the door. "Don said that you might stay for a little while, so we'll stop by quarters along the way."

"Thanks."

As we started down the corridor she said, "We don't get very many overnight guests here."

"Well, I can certainly understand that. If you'd picked a location nearer downtown, maybe close to an airport, advertise a pool or something—"

Her gaze stifled the rest of my response. Evidently she wasn't fond of being teased by someone she didn't know.

"Sorry," I said. "I get a little carried away sometimes. I needed a place to hide away for a while, and I found out that my sister Pat was here."

Her brown eyes softened a fraction, and I almost thought that the corners of her mouth crinkled.

"How much do you already know about this installation? I don't want to bore you with trivia that you might have heard before."

I couldn't foresee any boredom in my immediate future, but I didn't comment on that. "Not much. A few paragraphs of public-record description."

She picked a direction, and we began to walk. I already had the impression that I could very easily get lost in this place. The dimensions of the corridors were not a lot different from the halls back in my building, but the human engineering was far different.

The color-coded walls, direction markings, and floor-level indications present back home were almost entirely absent here. We had made several turns and passed through a few different corridors so far, and they all seemed virtually identical. It was as though the original builders had wanted infiltrators to have a hard time finding their way around. As if someone smart enough to find a way in would be dumb enough not to bring a map. Some of the intersections sported round, convex mirrors presumably meant to reduce the possibility of collisions.

We passed by a faded, ripped poster proclaiming, "I am your worst enemy—I am carelessness." Someone had crossed out "carelessness" and scrawled "RIF" in its place.

"You'll see an odd assortment of equipment in here," she said, noticing my glance through one of the few doors that was open. "This place got its start in the mid-nineteen hundreds and was actively being upgraded until the late two thousands. It's loaded with electronic, hydraulic, and mechanical systems. Some of them even lasted the life of the facility.''

"And newer systems were added?"

"Right. This place ran through over half a dozen generations of electronic and photonic equipment, including computer systems. With the typical cost reductions for each new generation of hardware, the salvage value of the installation was near zero. When they shut the place down, they just smashed a couple of classified systems but left most everything else intact. There never was much in the way of weapons. The facility was passive. They established it to monitor activities and send messages. It wasn't meant to participate in an offense, except to direct other sites.''

"Do you use many of the systems that were already installed when you got here?"

"No. The basic systems still provide things like power, light, and plumbing. And we made some minor modifications to the most recent generation of equipment. But most of what we use now is ours.''

"Are you tied into the main net?" I asked, thinking about contacting Seldon or Krongard.

"Yes. But not directly. We've got a few regular terminals back on the outside wired up to a short-burst neutrino transponder. Inside we've got a few repeater slave terminals tied to the transponder.''

"Fancy."

"Like I said, we wanted privacy.''

"Why? I mean, what are you doing that you need that much privacy?" I tried hard to make my voice casual, hoping that being Pat's brother might persuade her to tell me. No such luck.

"You can find out from Don, when and if he's ready to tell you.''

I could sense her retreating, not only in what she said, but also in her tone of voice. I moved back to an approved topic.

"So you're self-sufficient in here?"

"Yes. Power, food, light, air, water, for quite a while. We've got an old fusion generator along with enough raw materials to keep us comfortable indefinitely." She seemed more comfortable, too, now that the conversation had shifted back to a safer subject.

We hadn't seen any other people during our walk, but now I could see movement ahead.

"So there *are* other people in here," I said.

"That's the quarters area ahead. There are between one and two dozen buildings in here, but we actively use only about eight of them, and not the whole building in each case."

"My God. A dozen buildings this size?"

She looked puzzled for a moment but then said, "Oh, we haven't been in just one building. They're not *that* big. We've come through three or four buildings."

"But I don't remember leaving any building."

"They're joined. Remember those raised sections of floor, maybe three meters long? Those were EMP corridors."

"What?"

"Electromagnetic pulse. One of the secondary effects of a nuclear blast. The buildings are all shielded, and some of the entrances actually have EMP doors, but those corridors are an effective substitute—they're cavities that keep the energy from entering the buildings."

I was beginning to get a feel for the size of this place. I was also getting a calibration on Lisa.

As we talked my initial awareness of her as a person was complemented by my awareness of her as a woman. She, like Pat, wore no detectable makeup, but she didn't seem to need any. Lisa had the look of someone who got plenty of exercise without building bulging muscles.

Also she was sharp. Her knowledge of the installation didn't come falteringly, and at the same time, it obviously wasn't rehearsed. She had a relaxed manner that implied self-confidence. I kept thinking back to Krongard's statement, though. The one about an agent already in the facility. Who could it be, if he or she were still alive?

As we reached the quarters area a couple of people were leaving via a door at the far end, but Lisa didn't bother to call to them. One of them, an older woman, seemed familiar, but I couldn't remember from where. Maybe an older acquaintance of Pat's.

A secondary corridor split off from the main hall. Five or six doors down from the junction Lisa opened a door.

"You can stay here," she said. "We can get you some blankets later."

The room was bigger than my apartment, but didn't appear to have any of the mass-housing built-ins, so I guessed that it was intended primarily for sleeping. In general, most of the rooms that I had seen so far had been slightly larger than those back in my building.

Before I arrived, I would have bet that the rooms here would be even bigger, since the complex was built back when space was much less critical. Evidently the floor space this far into a granite mountain had been at a premium because of excavation costs. Either that, or most of the people who had worked here were clerical—which seemed unlikely.

We left the buildings for a while, wandering through tunnels as Lisa showed me some of the support equipment. There were reservoirs for cooling water and a reservoir for drinking water, each big enough to fill numerous Olympic-size pools, but close enough to the rock ceiling to prohibit diving. She showed me the fusion generator and remnants of the previous diesel generator. Blast valves protected the air intake from shock waves. Several filters provided protection from biological and radiological effects.

From there we went back into the buildings and continued exploring. I immediately became lost again. We saw the mess hall, a dispensary, several corridors barred by combination-lock doors, and room after room filled with ancient, dusty machinery. One multi-tiered room had the appearance of being the center of activities, with numerous flat panels that must have been status displays and rows of consoles, some apparently still using old plasma display panels.

"Aren't you getting a little tired yet?" I finally asked, near exhaustion.

"No, I'm fine. Sorry, I guess you're not used to this altitude."

"No. I guess not."

Actually there was no guessing required. We had gone up and down stairs, and twisted around some strange intersections between corridors. A person wouldn't have had to add very much to make the place a pretty good maze. Escher would have loved that place.

"You want to rest for a few minutes?" she asked. "You don't need to be embarrassed."

"Please."

Lisa opened a door and fumbled around for the light switch. She flipped it on and light spilled over dusty desks and file cabinets. The chairs had been removed, so we sat on a couple of the desks.

"How many people are here?" I asked after catching my breath.

"Enough to do the job. My charter was to show you around, not tell you what we're doing or what our resources are."

"Not even a hint?"

"More than five, less than five hundred." Lisa puffed her cheeks and then expelled the air slowly.

"Thanks. Can you at least tell me how long you've been here?" I asked.

"Over a year," Lisa replied after a brief hesitation.

"You've been inside all that time?"

She nodded.

"Doesn't that bother you some?"

"A little, but it's not all that different. How often do you go outside?"

"I don't know. Maybe every couple of months," I said.

Lisa tipped her hand over, palm up, as if to say, "So, there you have it."

"That's different. I could have gone out more often if I wanted to."

"So can I. I just need to be more careful."

"Careful?" I echoed.

"Not to use my wristcomp. The government knows by now that we're here, but there's no point in making things too easy for them. They probably don't yet have a complete list of who's here."

"If they know you're here, what's the point?"

"The point is that even if they know we're here, they still don't know what we're doing."

"And that is?"

"Sure is nice weather we're having lately."

"Well, then, what do you do for recreation?" I can pick up a subtle hint as well as the next person.

"There's a gym and a tennis court."

"A tennis court in here?"

"Well, almost. In the early two thousands they decided to put in another couple of buildings. They finished the excavation, and then the next administration decided that the project was too expensive. The area was almost large enough, so they put in the court surface and some lights. It's actually not too bad, if you can get used to not being able to lob as high as you normally can."

"How many people play?" I was genuinely curious, but I also thought I could extrapolate to the resident population, assuming that they were an average mix.

Lisa either saw through my question or was very protective about her sport. "At least enough for doubles."

"How often do you play? And is that a safe question?" I asked.

In partial answer Lisa made the flat-handed palm-down "safe" sign. "A couple of times a week. We keep busy, but a person has to have time to keep in shape. Once in a while, though, I wish there were a higher positive pressure in here. There's a slight gradient over the outside, but we're fairly high and the gradient isn't very much. At this altitude, it's still more effort than at sea level."

"I know." I was only then recovering from the tour around the facility. The buildings we had visited contained several corridors that for probably outdated reasons were blocked off. At least twice I had been sure that we had to go down and then up adjacent sets of stairs to visit two rooms that were separated by only five meters.

"It's not quite so bad after you get used to it," Lisa said.

"I hope you're right."

"It doesn't matter much. You might not be here that long."

"Exactly how long do you think that will be?"

"Probably about forty-eight hours minus ten minutes for each question that you ask," she said, and no smile softened the words.

"That's not at all encouraging."

"That's possibly because it wasn't meant to be. We don't have time to rent rooms, and our goals go beyond the convenience of a single person."

"Who's the decision up to? Don?" I asked.

"He has a say," she said, still not admitting any solid facts. "We'd better get back for dinner before you run out of time."

I didn't object, but it was then that I realized I didn't want the conversation to end. I wasn't learning much more about the complex, and it didn't appear likely that I would soon, but I was enjoying Lisa's company. She had an intangible quality that kept me alert and interested in what she was going to say next. Unfortunately on the trip to the mess hall she chose to say little.

I couldn't think of much more to ask that wouldn't make me sound like a reporter or a spy, so I didn't say much either. A few more faded posters clung to the walls at sporadic intervals. One of them warned me, "Don't be the weak link in the COMSEC chain." "Loose lips sink ships," was catchier, but I wasn't too surprised not to see any of those around.

Watching Lisa was more fun than reading old posters. She led the way when we passed through narrow corridors and up and down stairs. Her blond hair was long enough to sway as she turned her head. Her walk was slow and easy but not lazy. She wore casual clothes like Pat's.

I was almost winded again by the time we reached the mess hall. Twenty or thirty people were there already, but I didn't ask if that was the entire group. The selections in the cafeteria dispensers were mostly concentrates and instants. We joined Pat and Don at a table.

"What do you think of our surplus city?" Don asked, motioning us to sit.

"Very impressive. You probably have the most expensive suburb in the world. And no urban rot. My compliments to the city fathers."

"You toured the entire facility?" Don directed his question to Lisa.

"Most of areas one, two, five, and ten."

"There's more?" I asked, certain that there was.

"Yes, but not for your eyes, I'm afraid," he said.

"You're pretty quiet," I said to Pat.

She blinked before she spoke. "Sorry. I'm glad to see you but sorry that you can't work on the project with us."

"Don't be silly," I said. "I'm not that expensive."

"You know what I mean, Mike. In spite of the fact that I can vouch for you, you're not going to be admitted into the group."

"There's one other consideration also," Don added. "You don't know what's going on, so there's no way Brother Sammy can pump you for information. You know now that we're here, but they know that much already."

"Don't you even need a flunky?" I asked.

"Even if we did," he said, "the extra fuss of having to watch our conversations around you would be a net drain on our resources."

I gave up temporarily and resumed my meal. Krongard didn't strike me as the type of guy who would give me my job back if I returned to tell him that I was out of luck. He struck me as the type of guy who would strike me.

I glanced up to see Lisa's eyes looking in my direction. Her lips formed an embarrassed smile as she averted her gaze. Dammit. I wanted to be on the inside. If only I could tell them that I already had a good idea about the nature of their project. After all, I had spent plenty of time at a scapescope console. Surely that experience was worth something.

At that moment things fell into place. Thinking about scapescope triggered the image of the gray-haired woman I had seen in the quarters area.

"Celeste Newbury," I blurted out. Neither Don nor Lisa betrayed any reaction, but I saw Pat's eyes, and they were still easy to read.

"That was Celeste Newbury back there," I said, hoping that I'd found a way to get in. "I recognized her from the news reports. And if she's here, you've got to be working on something related to scapescope."

chapter
TWELVE

As soon as I mentioned Celeste Newbury's name and scapescope, everyone at the table became as quiet as a taxpayer during an audit. Don was the first one to speak after an uneasy pause. "There's no way to stop your speculations, but we still can't confirm or deny them."

He went back to his meal, apparently thinking about the situation. Evidently he wasn't one to bemoan past mistakes. By then there was little doubt that he was indeed the leader of the group.

I looked at Don. "I won't cause you any trouble," I said, hoping that it would be true.

A brief shadow crossed his face before he replied. "Let's be sure of that."

"I'm sure it'll be all right," Pat said, coming to my aid, maybe trying to reduce the tension.

Moments later Don excused himself and left the table. Lisa had said very little at dinner. I wondered if she were more comfortable with people who would soon be departing.

"How do you handle books and music in here?" I asked Pat to get the conversation back to a neutral topic. The speaker on my wristcomp was totally inadequate for the job, even if it weren't shielded from the main net. And reading just one chapter on its display would probably give me terminal eyestrain in more ways than one.

"We've got a couple of terminals hooked to repeaters that tie into the main net, but you won't be able to get access to them. You can use one of the local-node terminals. They're all tied to an internal computer that acts as an interface to the main net. You'll have most of the main capabilities, but not all."

"Which ones can't I have?" I asked.

"Message exchange, at least with anyone out of the local node. And most of the services that make entries in the data base, like reservations and purchases."

"So my wristcomp is now useless?"

"No, the complex is shielded so you can't get to the main net, but as soon as we put your ID into the local node, it'll recognize you." Pat pushed her hair away from her eyes again.

Her timing was good. I had decided it was time to ask another question, and I wanted to be able to see her eyes clearly. "So, you're working on a longer-range scape-scope?"

She must have realized from my glance that I wanted to see her expression, because she abruptly closed her eyes and put her hands up to her forehead. Both women were quiet for a long moment before Pat finally spoke.

"Mike, I can't tell you anything about the work in progress. Just accept that, okay?"

"All right. And I'm sorry." Sorry that I had hurt her, and sorry that I didn't know any more than before.

"Where were you before you came here, Lisa?" I

asked, trying to get her back into the conversation and to fall back to safer topics.

"The same complex as Pat, but in a different department. I was an applications engineer. We knew each other then, as you might have guessed. You'd have a winding path to follow, but if you traced who knew whom before we came here, you'd get to everyone here."

"Who knew Celeste Newbury?" I asked.

"Neither of us. She's a couple of friends removed," Pat answered. "No one you would know."

"She was one of the last to come," Lisa added. "Her disappearance was bound to cause the most disturbance."

"I take it she contributed even before she got here, though?"

"Yes." Lisa wouldn't elaborate.

At that moment I realized how my questions had been focusing on the project again. In their place I probably wouldn't need much fuel for paranoia. I also realized how tired I was. It had been a long day, and at an altitude much higher than what I was accustomed to.

"I think it's past my bedtime," I announced. "Could someone show me my quarters before I pass out?"

Pat volunteered. We didn't talk very much on the way, and I ran into only one wall-mounted fire extinguisher.

"How do I find my way to the mess hall tomorrow morning?" I asked once I was sitting in my new room.

"Don't worry about it for now. By then we'll have your ID in the local node," Pat said. "Call me on your wristcomp when you wake up, and I'll guide you there."

We talked for another few minutes, and she showed me where the nearby facilities were. After she said good night, I just sat on the bed in my room for another minute. Then, in spite of my exhaustion, I grabbed a robe and made my way into the community showers and spent twenty minutes under the water.

The thorough scrubbing probably eliminated any of Krongard's bugs that might still have been left on me. I made a mental note to get rid of my old clothes the next day. Before falling asleep I noticed a terminal in my room. At least I wouldn't have to unfold the keyboard in my compband.

Several anticlimactic days passed. My hope of being rapidly admitted to the inner circle faded, and my desire to see more of Lisa grew. She had retreated still more after the first night's dinner conversation.

I hadn't been introduced to any more people, but strangers in the corridors knew my name. In general, they were friendly but uncommunicative. I could find my way from quarters to the mess hall and back with solid-state reliability—as long as I kept close to the recommended path I was fine, but a few-meters sidetrack was enough to get me completely lost.

Mainly I was feeling useless. An urge to contribute was growing, partly because whatever they were doing was something Pat believed in, and partly because I needed to gain the knowledge that Krongard was after. Fighting the urge for involvement was another urge that was much less understandable to me. I didn't think of myself as lazy, but I could feel myself gaining inertia in my noninvolvement.

To be sure, nonparticipation wasn't all my fault. I had volunteered and been turned down several times. But I wasn't as persistent as I normally was when trying to attain an important goal.

It didn't help matters either to be in doubt about what

to do regarding Lisa. The remnants of pain left over from Sal flared and told me to mend my own fences and build my own barriers, but the quiet strength and compassion that I could read in Lisa's eyes compelled me to reassess.

Once I reassessed, I used one of my least-favorite decisions and applied it to this new case: Wait and see what develops. For all I knew, Lisa was working for Krongard.

The developing process continued that evening, but I couldn't tell yet if it would be a negative or a positive. I found out that Lisa played tennis at least an hour a day, and I managed to invite myself along.

We reached the court about an hour after dinner. Her regular partner or partners must have canceled, because we were the only two there. It felt strange not to have to pay for court time. The tunnel walls made the space feel more enclosed than the courts back home.

"Do you feel lucky tonight?" I asked, having absolutely no idea of what to expect.

"No more than usual," Lisa replied. "Why, do you think I'll need to be?"

"I hope so," I replied, watching her put on a headband and a wristband. She exuded confidence as she walked onto the court.

She gave me a racquet, and, partly to relax, I took my time adjusting the string tension, throat stiffness, and the grip circumference. I didn't bother to change the center of gravity much. The racquet felt good already. The osmosis sweat-trap was empty, so I was all set.

The first thing I noticed when we started hitting was that the balls I hit sailed long in spite of my attempts to keep them in the court. Lisa confirmed my guess that the lower air density at this altitude was responsible. My second observation was that the lower air pressure affected not only the balls. I was gasping for breath whenever I ran.

The third thing I noticed was that she was good. *I* was probably going to be the one to need the luck.

We finished warming up and started a set. Early in the first game I tried a lob over her head. It was too short, or her reach was too good, and the ball came zipping back past my right hip.

"Hey, you almost hit me," I said, feigning injury.

"Put your racquet in front of whatever you'd least like hit and cross your fingers."

I didn't comment on trying to cross my fingers and hold onto my racquet simultaneously. Her smile sometimes had a way of cutting off a conversation. We each held our serve in the first few games, but before long she broke my serve once and won six to four.

"Stupid game," I said, panting.

"Think of it as a character-building experience," Lisa said innocently.

"Stupid character-building game," I said, and trudged back onto the court.

The second set went pretty much the same, but I spent more time watching her. She could probably have beaten me much more soundly if she had wanted to.

I didn't think sports in general were truly character-building, but I did think that they could be used to gauge character that was already present. I fell back on one of the big three areas of male analogies and comparisons: sports, sex, and the military.

If the game were a reasonable analogy to life as a whole, Lisa was honest, stood up for herself when she was right, knew her own limitations and her strengths. If a ball was beyond her reach, she didn't waste her strength running after it, but if she had any reasonable chance, however tiny, she raced after it with tenacious enthusiasm. And she succeeded much more often than I would have guessed. I might have been able to learn more about her by watching how she reacted when she was losing, but for some reason I felt that she'd act just the same.

As I recuperated after an exhausting trouncing in the second set, I understood the padding that covered the bottom two meters of the tunnel walls. It was bad enough to have to have Lisa running me back and forth across the court; if I ran into one of those rock bolts or granite outcroppings, I'd certainly be a sore loser.

"You put up more of a struggle than I thought you would," Lisa said, relaxing and stretching.

"You should have told me you'd played before," I barely managed to squeeze out between gulps for air.

"Now I suppose you're going to tell me that you let me win."

"Did it show that much?" I flopped my arms over and started to laugh, but my ribs hurt too much. If we'd been playing outside, I would have got a sunburned tongue from all my panting.

"Are you sure you're all right?" she asked with a more serious tone.

"I'm fine. But if you're all that tired, maybe we shouldn't play a third set." Pain or not, I couldn't stop it any longer. For no reason that I could understand, I began laughing, slightly at first, then harder.

After a moment I heard Lisa laughing too. And then I was laughing even harder.

We were quiet on the way back. I didn't know what Lisa was thinking about, but I suddenly realized how long it had been since I had laughed like that.

I had always differentiated sports and games, games being played for fun, exercise, and enjoyment, while sports were for keen, finely tuned, fierce competition in which winning attained a much higher status. Lisa had the quality of being able to perform with sports-type effectiveness, while still maintaining the gamelike innocence that produced enjoyment and a spirit of fun.

Before we parted, I talked Lisa into showing me around more of the complex after she finished work the next night. She didn't resist the suggestion the way I somehow thought she might. That night I met her in the mess hall, and we started from there.

We began by touring some parts of the complex I hadn't seen before, but for most of the time Lisa and I walked through the sections that I knew. After taking several paths through the main area, I began to get a better feel for where things were. And where the boundary surrounding the limited-access area was.

Actually there seemed to be two off-limits areas. When questioned, Lisa admitted the larger area was their normal work area and that the other enclosure held a few extra terminals that were tied via a repeater to the main net. The only entry doors I saw were protected by combination locks.

When I asked another question concerning the nature of their work, she gave me the familiar "stop" sign. By that time I was getting tired again, so we sat down in a nearby stairwell.

"So that's it?" I asked. "I never will get to help out, or even find out what you're doing?"

"That's up to Don," she said, with a touch of a worried frown tugging at her features. "Why don't you just drop the subject, though? It won't be too long before we're finished."

That was the first information I'd heard about the timetable. I didn't push any more, but it occurred to me that the pressure to acquire information had just in-

creased. I hated to put Lisa in a hard position by press-
ing her for details she was prohibited from divulging,
but I couldn't very well ask Don, and I was afraid that if
I spent enough time with Pat she might see through my
façade.

We talked more before it got too late. Most of the
topics were innocuous, but I had a good time. Lisa was
fun to talk to without being talkative. If the conversation lagged or she thought of another interesting idea,
she moved on, but she always left plenty of time for me
to respond or to perform my own change of subject.

I liked a conversation that challenged my mind but
not my powers of interruption. And it was nice to have
a conversation in which there was no need to be the
loudest to receive attention.

We said good night, and I watched her as she took the
corridor to her quarters. Lisa was one nice lady.

Sleep came very slowly that night. I had as many
questions as I had when Sal found my name on the list,
and now there was no scapescope to help me answer any
of them.

That night I dreamed about Lisa and scapescope. In
my dream I had access to an improved scapescope that
could answer almost any question put to it, but I didn't
use it. Every time I was about to turn it on, something
came up and I never got a chance to ask it some of my
burning questions. At least I didn't get any burning
answers.

The next morning, more to pass the time than anything else, I tried out the terminal in my room. It was an
old model, but it had all the essential features. I was
glad that I had turned it on. The local-node data base
had more complete information on the layout of the
complex.

The best part was that the data base included detailed

maps of every building and all floors. The maps were thorough. They showed details down to the level of air-conditioning ducts and electrical and optical cables.

They also showed something else. Something even more interesting.

On the roofs of some of the buildings there were rectangular shapes, each containing what looked like a wheel lock. And if they were indeed emergency-access doors, they might allow entrance to both of the restricted areas. The color-coding indicated they weren't original equipment but had been added later.

The drawings also showed the locations of ladders on the outside walls of four or five of the buildings. I filed the information away. There was no way I could afford to be caught snooping around right then. But I always felt better having options.

Once I knew my way around better, I spent even more time wandering around the public areas of the installation. I must have spent at least as much time in the tunnels as in the buildings. I was so accustomed to the constant gentle rumbling that I noticed it only occasionally. The lights were left on all the time, so, just like home, night never existed except as a set of digits on a clock.

During my walks I noted the locations of all the ladders, but I didn't try them. They did seem to be afterthoughts rather than original equipment, but it was hard to tell.

Whenever I walked in the tunnels, I had to watch out for water dripping from the tunnel ceiling. Lisa had explained about the rock bolts. Some of them were wedge bolts from two to ten meters long, inserted into holes drilled in the granite and then tightened. Once secure, they compressed a layer of rock that provided increased protection for the occupants.

The bolts that I avoided were the grouted bolts, similar to the wedge bolts, but bored out so they could form a passage for excess underground water to escape. Most of it escaped from the ceiling bolts, so, except for the areas covered with foam or plasteel, the bolts provided a multitude of drips and puddles.

I spent hardly any time with Pat. She kept very busy, and I was still worried about her reading more into my questions than I cared for her to do.

As for Krongard, there was no way to communicate with him without getting access to the terminals that were tied into the main net. It was just as well. I wasn't at all eager to talk to him. If I had any options, they weren't obvious to me yet. And I wanted to have at least one more option than those known to Krongard.

I did get to see more of Lisa. She seemed to be experiencing a gradual thaw, punctuated by occasional lapses or retreats. I sensed that maybe she, too, had been hurt in the not-too-distant past, but I didn't pry.

I had plenty of time to relax, but I couldn't. That is, I spent a few more days on a leisurely schedule, but I wasn't calm. Not knowing what the group was trying to do, not wanting to hurt Pat or, now more than ever, Lisa, and not wanting to be on the government dirt list for life, all resulted in knots in my stomach.

Having little success in determining the logical ways out forced me to investigate the physical ways out. That search went quickly. There apparently were only two exits from the mountain complex. Three if you counted dying. And I didn't.

Neither exit could be used without assistance, however, so I abandoned that search.

I was almost stir-crazy by the time things started happening.

At dinner I saw Don for the first time in several days.

He was sitting with Pat and Lisa, and he waved me over. We all made small talk for a few minutes, but I detected a tension that had not been apparent previously.

"Something that we did not anticipate has happened," he said finally. "We've got a problem, and it appears that your skills would help us overcome it more quickly than if we handled it solely with existing staff."

"What kind of problem?" I asked, barely able to restrain myself.

"There's no point in discussing it yet. You'll need some more education before it will make sense. The main question is, will you help?"

"Of course," I replied instantly. Anything to end the dull routine. I took my eyes off Don just long enough to glance at Pat and Lisa. They both reflected what seemed to be nervous relief.

"Well, then," Don continued, "in that case, I think it's time we told you what we are doing here."

chapter
THIRTEEN

Don's announcement came so suddenly, I could hardly believe it. I was finally going to learn the nature of the project. Again I scanned the faces of my dinner companions. Lisa's lips were almost imperceptibly pinched in apparent concern about my reaction. Surely she wouldn't think that I would refuse to help.

Pat, too, had an intense hardening of her features. Don's face was the inscrutable one. His expression told me no more than a deliberately farcical mouth-only smile presented to an antagonist, probably the result of a similar conscious attempt to render me unable to gather information from any source other than his words.

While I had been examining the three of them, they had been watching me. At last Don spoke again.

"You've probably guessed the direction our efforts have taken. Celeste's presence here narrows the possibilities appreciably. It's fairly simple. Our work has been directed at the development of a longer-range scape-scope—one with a two-year span."

Two years. Krongard figured maybe one year.

"Two years," I said out loud. "That's fantastic. I thought noise in the field was responsible for a theoretical limit."

"So did we, for a long time. We've been wrong before and we'll probably be wrong again. You know as well as we that the only sure thing is change."

"Why?"

"Why?" he echoed.

"Why do it up here? Surely the government would be behind you all the way. They could provide all the experts you'd ever need. Why all the secrecy?"

"Because we're not interested in giving this to the government. All it would do is let Brother Sammy squeeze that much harder on private enterprise. Even someone with no background in economics or finance should be able to see that, by the end of the century, Brother Sammy will be the only employer in the Western Region."

I didn't reply immediately. The response that came almost automatically to my lips died. Before this whole mess started I certainly hadn't seen anything wrong with the government's size, but now that I could wind up on the outside for a long while, I couldn't tell if I was tasting sour grapes or if I actually sympathized with Don.

But, all things considered, it couldn't hurt to agree with him for the moment.

"Okay. So what do you want me to do?"

"First you'll need some specialized training." He took a brief look at his wristcomp before continuing. "I've arranged for it, and I expect it will take you three or four days to absorb it. It's set up in the local-node data base under the file name MC-PHOTONICS-CAI. You'll have permission by the time you try to access it."

"You want me to start now?"

"Tomorrow morning is soon enough. This problem

has a couple of cousins that some others of us need to solve.''

"Two years," I said again. "I still haven't adjusted. The avenues a time span like that will open. False starts will almost be extinct. Research efficiency should soar." Another thought distracted me. "And you must know already that it'll be successful, since you're close."

Don hesitated. "Well, actually we don't. The theoretical indications are virtually indisputable, but we can't use scapescope to predict the results, because the change won't occur instantaneously. There will be a four-year period during which the range will slowly increase from six months to two years."

"So you won't know until shortly after your device, or whatever you're developing, is tested?" Comprehension came to me slowly. The concept of not knowing the probable outcome until after a project's completion was a strange one to me.

"That's right," Don said.

I realized that Lisa and Pat had dropped out of the conversation. I had been waiting so long to hear words like the ones Don spoke, I had focused my attention on him alone, and the women had let him tell the whole story.

"So how do you two fit in?" I asked, glancing first at Lisa and then at Pat.

"There's time enough for that later," Don said. "Their jobs won't even make sense to you until you've learned more."

I asked a couple more questions, which Don also intercepted, before deciding that he strongly wanted me to wait until I learned more about the technical aspects of the job. With so much to think about, I excused myself from the table and roamed through the corridors for a while as I thought about the situation. I felt strangely confused. Instead of being comforted by an expected conclusion, I was as ill at ease as before.

The difference was that earlier I had been uneasy because of not knowing what was going on, but now I couldn't isolate the cause of my anxiety. Maybe I was concerned about not being smart enough to do whatever job they wanted done. Or possibly I was afraid of approaching the point at which I would have to decide between Krongard and the group.

I couldn't forget that Sal had chosen her career when faced with a similar decision. I caught myself before carrying that line of thought any further.

I knew it was oversimplification. Probably I had been doing the same thing in a variety of situations. I wasn't sure, but maybe when anyone underwent emotions as strong as the ones that had numbed me when Sal left, oversimplification would be a natural reaction. Like someone momentarily deafened by a thunderclap, my perceptions had been swamped. For a while I could only distinguish loud and soft, bright and dark. Maybe my ability to distinguish shades of gray was returning.

I was thinking about Sal a lot less frequently, but slowly I was beginning to understand that her departure had probably been triggered by a last straw rather than an isolated event. There had been other problems with the relationship. Problems I created, problems she created, and problems with our interactions. Maybe what actually bothered me most was her lack of faith in me.

My thoughts were beginning to bog down, darting from topic to topic and not staying on any particular one. Sal, Lisa, scapescope, the secrecy, Krongard—what made sense, and what didn't? Maybe talking to Lisa, forcing myself to verbalize, would help.

I found her in her quarters.

"Could I talk to you for a little while?" I asked, still

unable to read her expression.

"It's not going to make any more sense until you've had the extra training. I don't know what more to say."

"Forget about the technical details. I don't care about them. I'd just like to talk to you for now."

In answer she raised her hands over her head as if to a mugger, shrugged, and joined me in the hall. "Where?"

"Now wait a minute. If this is 'audience with the queen' time, maybe I'd be better off not bothering you."

"Let me make sure I have this right," Lisa said, with obvious impatience in her tone. "You want to impose, but you don't want to feel like you're imposing. Is that about it?"

"No, I—" I fumbled for a moment. "Well, yes, dammit. Aren't you ever wrong? I mean—what I'm trying to say is, I didn't want to impose, but I didn't expect this would be such a big deal. There's too much going on. I'm confused and I thought it might help to talk with you. But if you'd really rather not, I'll let you alone and quit bothering you. Fair enough?"

Her eyes scanned mine for a long moment, and then a few of the lines in her face relaxed and faded. "I'm sorry, Mike. I'd be glad to talk. I guess I'm a little tense tonight too."

"Why should you be tense? I'm the one who's being admitted to the inner circle."

"It's too complicated for now. I've got problems on my end of the project. Let's just leave it at that, all right?"

"You're sure?"

She made a "stop" sign with her hand, but a wry smile softened the edge.

"Okay," I said. "Mine may be complicated, too, though. I really don't know exactly what it is that I want to talk about or what it is that's bothering me."

"You've got to start somewhere," she said, and began walking slowly down the corridor toward the stairwell.

We took our time walking, made a few random turns, and arrived at an outside door. The air in the tunnel was chilly and the deep rumbling was more noticeable since I hadn't been outside for a while. I still hadn't figured out where to start.

"You're sure you wanted to *talk*?" Lisa's grin warmed me in spite of the cool air.

"Yes," I said, and grinned back. "Thanks." We sat down on the steps and I spent another thirty seconds thinking.

"I still don't know where to start," I said. "I'm like someone who has wanted a new, supercharged, left-handed frammis for a long time and can suddenly afford one. Instead of rushing out to buy one, he realizes that, with the knowledge of being able to afford one, his criteria have changed. I've waited for this time, but I must not have expected to get this far, and now that I'm here, I realize I haven't actually been asking myself the right questions about how I feel."

"How you feel about what?"

"I don't know. A lot of things. Whether or not I'll be able to learn enough to help. What kind of effects a two-year scapescope will have on people." I consciously left out one of my questions.

"There's not much you can do about the situation, so why spend a lot of time worrying?"

"Not worry? Not do one of the things I do best? Think of my self-image."

"Sorry. I lost my head." Lisa joked with me, but she still seemed much more nervous than before.

"Actually I don't see it as worrying. It's more like constructive concern. I don't like surprises." I looked back at Lisa. "Well, let's say I don't like most surprises."

"Then it seems that a two-year scapescope would be ideal for you," she replied, ignoring the compliment.

"Yeah. It's great for the long-range planner. What are you doing for dinner the forty-second Saturday of next year? I still don't know what I'm trying to say. I just feel unsettled."

"You're sure this isn't a medical problem?"

"Take two housecalls and see me in the morning? No. Maybe I should walk you back. I'm not getting anywhere."

"That's all you think about?" Lisa asked innocently.

"You know very well what I meant," I said, and grinned. "I guess I just need to drop the subject and let my subconscious work on it for now."

I stood up and brushed the dust off my pants. The return trip was quiet. I didn't understand the apparent change in Lisa. In previous conversations, she had shown a marked perception and an ability to draw out a person in conversation, and usually she illuminated formerly dark areas. Tonight she had simply reacted, responding to actual or implied questions, but not expanding on them or suggesting new directions for the discussion.

I attributed it to the fact that she was tense for her own reasons. Sometimes it was fun that women were such mysterious personalities. Sometimes it wasn't.

When we got back to her room, I said good night and then walked to my room. I stared at the ceiling for over a half hour, still trying to see how all the pieces fit together. Until then I had thought my empty feeling would disappear if I was accepted into the group, but the emptiness was still there.

I slept in my clothes. My thoughts simply wouldn't

quiet down until I was too exhausted to move.

In the morning I managed to formalize a couple of questions that called for answers. First, why shouldn't the government get the device, or how would they use it any differently than anyone else? And second, what effects would it have?

The latter question was a new one for me, but after thinking about it for a while, I was surprised that I hadn't asked it before.

I didn't have much time to think about the questions, though. Don called me for an early breakfast.

I found him and Pat in the cafeteria. Pat looked as tired as I felt.

"Are you okay?" I asked her.

"Sure. We've just had some late sessions, working on this latest problem." She gave me a bleak smile.

"So we start today?" I asked, wishing I felt more alert.

"Right," Don said. "We'll go up to the lab when we're finished here."

The lab had to be in one of the restricted areas, and I could guess which one. I was the last to finish breakfast, and when I was done, the three of us left. The lab turned out to be the restricted area on the first floor.

Pat gave me the combination to the lock as we went in. She left us there. The area inside the door looked pretty much the same as the other portions of the complex except for one large bay crammed with more electronic and photonic instruments than any lab I had been in before. There were so many pieces of equipment, I probably could have turned off the overhead lights and found my way around just using the light from all the displays and readouts.

On one long table there lay three scapescope terminals with their card cages exposed. All around the room were individually locked cabinets. Even if I had made my way in alone, I might not have come away with any useful information.

"Why all the security up here, when the only people inside are in on the project?" I asked.

"Not everyone knows all there is to know about the project," Don replied. "Everyone at least knows his assigned task, but not everyone knows all the details."

"Why?"

"Two reasons. One is economy of time; an individual can get up to speed in his own area much quicker than he can grasp the entire project. The other reason is security. We don't want the government to be able to get to one fringe member and obtain the entire process."

"So I'm not going to learn everything, either?"

"No. I'm afraid not. Does that bother you?" Don's eyes made me uncomfortable.

"I guess it doesn't yet."

We reached the work area that Don had been moving toward. He picked up a mil-standard circuit card, two by four centimeters.

"This is the critical board," he said. "It's the only significant difference between a regular scapescope and the new model."

I examined it briefly, but it had no distinguishing marks to indicate that it was anything special. The rough surface meant the card was densely populated, because cards that held less than a billion components could usually be laid down in a single layer.

"So what's the problem?" I asked again.

"We have to make a trade-off between layout and function. One of the peripheral components needs access to more data than it gets already. So we either need to do a redesign of almost a fifth of the board, or we need to cut down the frequency slices so we can multiplex more signals on the main optical data bus."

"No other choices?" I asked. My hands-on engineering skills had atrophied somewhat during the last few years with Brother Sammy, and the job sounded like a reasonably challenging one.

"You tell us after you've got into the problem. Here are most of the things you'll need. There are several duplicates of that card stored over here." Don motioned toward one of the locking file cabinets. "There are three copies of the design document in the bin on the top shelf, and they're in standard form. You can see the instruments by just looking around the room. There's a terminal in the corner and the CAI package is already loaded. Can you think of anything else you'll need?"

"Not for now. You seem pretty thorough."

"Fine. I'm sure you'll be busy for a while with the training material, but when you're ready, I'll introduce you to the people you'll be dealing with. Any last questions?"

"No. Thanks."

Don nodded and drifted off to another part of the lab. At least he gave the impression of aimlessly wandering, but I felt certain that he knew exactly what he wanted to do next and had a few questions or statements ready to use. What I was *uncertain* of was what he did for relaxation. I couldn't form any mental picture of him engaged in frivolous activity. A mental picture of him laughing at a joke somehow seemed incongruous.

I swung back to the terminal and loaded the CAI lessons. The first fifty frames were mostly a review, but then my pace dropped as the instruction modules started covering more and more new material. By lunchtime I had a good start on a case of mental fatigue. By the end of the day I had a matched set.

I quit as soon as someone else left. This just wasn't the type of work I could do for long hours. To make matters worse, I felt stupid because of having such a hard time with some of the lessons.

I beat Lisa to the mess hall, but she joined me when she got there. She looked tired again. I questioned her about it, but she wasn't much more communicative than she had been the day before. Her newly strengthened reserve puzzled me.

I ate quietly while thinking. Everyone probably had some type of shell. Some shells were more or less visible than others and the thicknesses varied considerably, but they were almost always present. I looked up at Lisa, but I didn't watch her long enough to attract her attention. Nearly everything about her made me think that she was someone genuinely worth making an effort for, but I was getting so tired of shell games.

Sometimes her conscious and unconscious barriers made me want to lower mine more, and possibly cause hers to fall. Other times I felt like strengthening my shell to protect myself. It was always easier to be the first to back off to avoid becoming the injured party.

I took another quick glance at her. I couldn't read anything in her posture or expression. *Dammit,* I told myself. *Quit being so analytical.* I tried to shut off my thoughts by restarting the conversation.

"It was a long day," I started, unsure of what I was going to say next. "But it feels good to be able to contribute. You must be pretty happy to finally be so close to the goal."

"Yes."

"Would you rather I leave you alone?" Again it would be less painful if I suggested it rather than waiting for her to say it.

"No," Lisa said quietly, softening. "I'm sorry I'm not very good company right now, but I'm not angry at you."

"Any problems I can help with?"

She took a deep breath before she said, "No, but that

doesn't mean I'd rather you were somewhere else. I'm glad you're here. Is that enough?"

"That's plenty." I managed to grin and coax a weak smile from her before I went back to my food. I felt better and was able to avoid analyzing why.

A long, solitary walk after dinner burned up some of my nervous tension, but I was still hyperactive when I got back to my room. And the visitor who interrupted my thoughts later that night didn't help one bit.

I had just about decided to go to bed when someone knocked quietly. For a wishful moment I hoped that it was Lisa, but it wasn't.

The person standing in the hall when I opened the door was a short, swarthy fellow whom I vaguely remembered being introduced to as Leon something-or-other. Leon Rubotto.

"Yes?" I said, puzzled by his presence.

"May I come in, Mr. Cavantalo?"

"What's this about?"

"I really think I should come in." His voice iced over. He struck me as the functional equivalent of a piece of one-way glass—only admitting light and warmth, but never transmitting any back out.

I motioned for him to enter and he closed the door behind him.

"I need to talk to you about a person named Krongard," he said, transferring the ice in his voice to my blood.

"Who?" I asked in my best imitation of nonchalance.

"I don't have a lot of time, Mr. Cavantalo. I know that you're an infiltrator working for him."

chapter
FOURTEEN

"What exactly makes you think that I even know anyone named Krongard?" I asked my unexpected visitor. My thoughts whirled in circles, going nowhere.

"Like I said before, I don't have time for any games," Leon replied. "I know you're working for Krongard because I am too."

Until that time I had been standing. My knees and stomach suddenly decided that I would be much better off sitting, so I did. Leon moved closer, his hooked nose making him look like an eagle. A belligerent eagle. His dark, piercing eyes heightened the effect.

"Look," I said, stalling. "Supposing, just supposing, mind you, that I did know this Krongard person and was somehow working for him, why should I believe you when you say you work for him too?"

"In that case, I suppose I'd need to provide proof that I know what I'm talking about. I might have to tell you that, for instance, I know the real reason you're on the wanted list."

Whatever Leon's job was, he obviously enjoyed it, because he almost glowed as he went on to tell me the real reason and describe the briefing session with Krongard with enough detail to convince me that he had been given the same briefing.

"Okay, okay," I said finally. "But Krongard told me he hadn't heard recently from anyone inside. How do you explain that?"

"Simple. He's a crafty bastard. He never shows anyone the whole picture when a glimpse will do. Security was tightened up here too. It's easier to receive messages than to send them out."

I had almost adjusted to the unpleasant fact that someone else inside knew why I was here, but what bothered me more was the conviction that soon my list of available options was probably going to shrink severely.

"All right. So you know Krongard and you know I work for him too. Now what?" I couldn't see anything to gain by protesting at that point. And the time didn't seem right to mention the fact that I felt queasy about the whole idea of helping Krongard, regardless of who would benefit.

"I need some help from you." Leon's tone didn't imply need, but insistence. The ice in his voice seemed even colder than before. "I want you to bring me one of the prototype boards and a copy of the design document."

"Your timing is good, at least. Today was the first time I had access to them."

"I was aware of that," he said dryly.

"How? How many of us are here?" I used the word "us" uneasily.

"You already know as much as you need to. Just get me the materials and I'll take care of getting them outside."

"I'm not sure I can get one without anyone noticing," I lied, trying to give myself more options and more time to think.

"I think you'd better." His eyes locked on mine for a moment, but he said no more, and I felt very little like asking him to elaborate.

"Well, I'll have to do some checking. If I take one and it's noticed ten minutes later, we've got problems. Right?"

He acquiesced grudgingly. "All right. But you'd better be quick. As soon as you have it, enter a note in the blind-drop file on the local node, addressed to 'Qwerty.' I'll put in a permanent scan for it, and I'll meet you here at 2100 the day it appears."

"Before you go—why does Krongard want the board? He can't put it to use yet. It's not functional."

"You'll find out if you need to know," Leon said. "Don't worry about it."

Great. Now I had another person telling me not to worry. He left before I could ask him any other questions.

Telling me not to worry is like telling a hunchback to stand at attention. Coming up: one more sleepless night. I knew I wouldn't sleep that night until I was simply too tired to avoid it, so I keyed in several requests for music. At least I might get a little enjoyment while awake.

It was hard to believe that my life had become so complicated. Before this all started, I went to work, came home, did things with Sal, enjoyed my music and books, slept, and hardly ever worried. Now I had an ample supply of things to worry about, a long list of questions, and a short list of answers.

I couldn't even keep my worries straight. Several times, right in the midst of worrying about being caught between Krongard and the group, a strong image of Lisa came to me. What did she really think about me, beneath all those layers of protection? Should I confide in her about Leon? How not to get hurt and how not to hurt anyone else? And was it even possible?

Another thought occurred to me, one of those thoughts that I tried harder and harder to suppress, unsuccessfully. If it hadn't been for scapescope, I'd probably still have my job. I couldn't stop the thought, but I did try to keep reminding myself that such a suspicion was not a valid reason for making a decision.

A fitful sleep finally came to me. When I woke, my eyes were still burning and I dreaded trying to spend a full day at the terminal.

As I stepped into the hall and closed my door behind me, I contemplated breakfast. My stomach didn't feel even slightly hungry, and it grew even more queasy as the idea of talking with Lisa came to mind. It would be a terrific conversation if I confessed to working for Brother Sammy. That would be a great way to bring down the barriers.

Unsure of what to do and what not to do, I decided to skip breakfast and just sidestep the situation. By 1100 I was so hungry I broke for an early lunch. It wasn't until I went back to the lab after eating that I realized I had maneuvered myself into missing Lisa a second time.

The more I thought about it, the more reasons I came up with for continuing to avoid her. Not seeing her would be good in that I wouldn't have to try to conceal my confused thoughts. If she were cooling to me, it would be less painful just to stop seeing her rather than be told to stop. And if she weren't, maybe she'd seek me out.

My thoughts sometimes wandered throughout the afternoon. Occasionally they returned to the cause of the whole chaotic question: scapescope.

The sounds of several people leaving the lab at 1700 lurched me out of an almost trancelike state. Triggered by the jolt, my thoughts coalesced and, the way it sometimes happened to me, I knew that I had a plan of action.

There were a couple of initial steps to take, but by tomorrow or the next day I would have a message for Leon.

The first order of business was to figure out how to get access to one of the regular terminals that were tied into the main net. I needed information and I had to get it privately. Daytime hours were out. Every function I legitimately required for my assigned job was available on the local-node system. So I would have to use one of the outside lines when no one would be around to notice.

Before I left the lab, I casually strolled around, looking for indications that the area contained some main-net terminals. A locked room within the lab was the only possibility, but it would be virtually impossible to enter. That meant I'd have to try the third-floor restricted area, which was still off-limits to me. The knowledge was disconcerting, but I remembered something possibly helpful. Unfortunately it would have to wait until later that night.

I still felt uncomfortable with the idea of seeing Lisa, so I went back to my room until a half hour after the mess hall should have been empty. After a quick journey I grabbed enough of a snack to appease my appetite. It took very little appeasing. I was too tense to eat much.

Waiting four hours until most people would be out of the halls was almost the hardest part. I selected some somber music, hoping for relaxation, but it had little effect that night. I kept imagining being caught in the process of executing my plan. None of the possible consequences seemed pleasant.

When it was time, I quickly made two hard copies on my room terminal and stuffed them into my pocket. I remembered just as I was leaving my room to turn off the audible alarm on my wristcomp. If anyone called, the visual would suffice, and I didn't want to risk the noise. I punched a couple more commands into the room terminal and left.

I gave my impression of a stroll as I made my way out to one of the tunnels. My insomnia excuse was all prepared, but no one showed up to force me to use it. The corridors were as quiet as I had hoped they would be. The tunnel also was empty.

The odds were good that no one else would just happen to be out for a walk, but I didn't waste any time. One of the ladders that I had noticed earlier chilled my hands as I climbed it. I tried to keep my steps as light as I could. The metallic construction of the building could easily carry more noise and vibrations than I wanted.

In spite of the air filtration system in the complex, the roof was thick with grimy dust. I would have to trust that no one would be up here for periodic checks. I'd never be able to cover up the indications of my visit.

The irregular ceiling of the cavern came low enough in places to make me crouch. The edges of the roof were brightly lighted, so I wasn't worried about falling off, but I almost tripped over the wheel protruding from the section of roof that interested me. It wasn't quite as grimy as the building surface itself since some of the grit that landed on its handle could roll off and fall to the plane of the roof, but it was still filthy. I took off a sock to use as a dust cloth. If I were able to get inside, I certainly didn't want to leave a trail of dirty doorknobs. And who's been using my doorknob, Goldilocks asked, I thought crazily.

I took a deep breath to keep the sound of my breathing from interfering with my hearing, and I gave the wheel a very gentle twist. No response.

I tugged at the wheel again, harder this time. It moved. With a streak of good luck that had been absent from my life all too long, the wheel continued to turn under my hands without squeaking. A half dozen rotations brought the handle to the stop.

I resumed breathing while I pondered what might lie below. Taking another deep breath, I slowly lifted the hatch cover, almost expecting to see a roomful of people.

I was wrong, naturally. Below was nothing but darkness. I locked the cover in the upright position and pointed my flashlight into the gloom. My luck was still holding.

The room below appeared to be a small storeroom, no larger than a couple of closets stuck together. It seemed unlikely to be a high-use room. Also in my favor, a stack of sturdy-looking boxes was close to my entrance. I hooked the light onto my belt and dropped to the floor. The fall didn't bother me, but the abrupt stop stung my soles. I shoved the pile of boxes closer to the opening. They were heavy, but the floor was clean, so they slid without too much trouble. I climbed on top of them.

From there, I could just reach the cover to close it. My heart slowed as I sat down in my sanctuary, the hatch cover sealed and my body shielded from the door.

I was still surprised that I had been able to get in. The only sensible explanation was that the group felt secure enough inside the complex that they weren't as thorough with internal security checks as they should have been. That is, if I were actually in the area housing the extra main-net terminals. The use of this area remained questionable.

Another few moments were enough to let me collect my thoughts and relax, but I was still tense when I rose and prepared to try the door. A soft band of light on the floor implied a lighted corridor beyond. That wasn't necessarily a sign of trouble. The hall lights were on twenty-four hours a day.

I pulled on the door until I could see through the narrow crack. Just a bare wall in that direction. After a minute of listening I decided that no one was nearby. I craned my neck out of the doorway and read the room number. With the door closed again, I dug out the hard copies I had made back in my room. I unfolded them and found the map I needed.

More good news. The room I was in had been my target, which meant there must be one room to my left, across the hall, and three more to my right. I chose the largest one as my first candidate. If the door was locked, I still might be able to travel from one room to another by removing hanging-ceiling squares, but that approach would be my last choice. After another delay while I made sure that the corridor was still empty, I left the relative safety of the storeroom. I padded quietly down the hall, noticing as I went that all four rooms had their doors closed and all were apparently dark.

I hesitated in front of the door to the large room, afraid that for some reason it might be occupied. The realization that I would be instantly exposed to anyone entering the area via the main door at the end of the hall overcame my inertia. The door was unlocked. I opened it slowly, edged my way into the dark, and shut the door behind me.

It was still as silent as it was dark, so I switched on the light. More luck. Three terminals lined the far wall. I turned off the light.

Feeling safer in the darkness, I shuffled over and sat down at the far terminal. A couple of file cabinets would provide some concealment in the event of unexpected visitors. I just hoped I would hear them coming down the hall.

A blaze of light startled me as I turned the terminal on. The brightness was set for a lighted room, so I dimmed it until I could barely see the text. I had my

message text prepared. Since it was in the code that
Seldon and I had agreed on, I couldn't type the non-
sense syllables rapidly, so I had typed it on my room terminal and patched the text over to my wristcomp. Now I
patched the apparently meaningless phrases into the
main-net terminal.

Two obstacles could conceivably slow down the
answer to my query. First, the variable delay on the
transmitted and received messages as they were routed
through the blind-drop site. Second, it might take Seldon a little while to determine the answer and encode his
reply. After I transmitted the message, I could have
signed off and gone back to my room before a return
trip, but I decided to wait in case the response came
quickly. No sense risking a second visit.

I curled up behind the cabinets and waited, listening
for the beep of an incoming message. A quiet rush of air
from the ventilator made the only noise I heard during
the wait, but I was still worried about being found there.
Explaining my presence would be about as easy as
changing an adult's religious convictions.

After one hour that seemed like five, a soft beep summoned me from my resting place. I couldn't tell from
looking at the text if it was the answer I was hoping for,
but it seemed longer than a simple, "I don't know."

I patched the message into my wristcomp. I could
decode it back in the relative safety of my room.

"Thanks, Seldon," I whispered fervently, and signed
off. I turned the brightness back up to its original level
and switched off the terminal.

The hall was still deserted when I poked my head out
of the door. I tiptoed back down to the door of the storage room and entered. Finally I began to feel less anx-
ious, but I had to get back to my room before relaxing.

My arms hurt as I pulled myself up through the hatch.
Fortunately the junction between the hatch and its cover

was clean, so I didn't pick up any more grease. Shortly I was back on the floor of the tunnel, with almost all traces of my visit removed. I stuffed the greasy sock behind a rock-bolt cover so high that I had to stretch to reach it.

Inside at last, I felt much better. Even if I did meet someone, my "couldn't sleep" excuse should certainly suffice.

I was impatient to read Seldon's reply, but that would have to wait. Once inside my room the first thing I did was take my room terminal out of record mode and initiate a maximum-db scan.

Good. The loudest noise level in my room during my absence was under eighteen decibels, softer than a whisper. So no one had knocked or called me, and therefore I didn't need to worry about any excuses about sleeping soundly or being gone.

There was one final task to perform before I could sleep. I lined up the photodiode on my wristcomp with the receiver on my room terminal and beamed Seldon's message over. It didn't take long for me to type in the decoding sequence. I pressed the return key and leaned back.

The local-node computer translated the message faster than I could read it. As tired as I was, I would have gone back to the main-net terminal to send Seldon a thank-you if it hadn't been for the risk involved. He told me all I needed to know.

I slept soundly that night, but I had so little time in bed that I could barely struggle out when the alarm sounded. I skipped breakfast and went straight to the lab. Probably no one would immediately miss an extra set of notes on the prototype, but to stall the discovery of the disappearance of the board I was stealing, I located an outdated version, obscured the revision number, and left it in place of the real one.

At no time during the morning was I alone in the lab for more than a minute, but that afternoon I had over ten minutes when several people took a break together. It was all the time I needed for one last task. When I was finished, I posted the message to Leon's coded box name. Now for the wait until 2100.

Backing down from my decision to avoid Lisa, I decided to at least say, hi, briefly at dinner. I wasn't entirely sure why I changed my mind except for the fact that I had missed seeing her. I still didn't know if it were the right thing to do, but it turned out to be a moot question.

Lisa wasn't in the mess hall. I managed to cut off my worry that maybe *she* was now avoiding *me*. I could worry about things I was more knowledgeable about and had more influence over.

Twenty-one hundred finally arrived, closely followed by a knock on my door. I opened it and admitted Leon.

"Well, where are they?" he asked, his glare making me feel shorter than I was.

A remnant of indecision slowed me briefly; I dug the prototype and notes out of their meager concealment and placed them in his hands. I didn't feel up to talking.

He gave them a cursory examination before he tapped a few keys on his wristcomp, possibly to tell his accomplice or accomplices that they had been successful.

"You do real good work, Cavantalo," he said, the tone in his voice almost mocking, sarcasm instead of congratulation in his manner.

"You sound as if you don't want it."

"I don't care about it," he replied. "But someone else is very interested in it." Even as he spoke, he opened the door.

And in walked Don.

chapter
FIFTEEN

"You're a big disappointment," Don said to me, "but at least we found out now rather than later."

I was still too stunned to reply. The shock of seeing him was too much to handle for the moment. He used my silence as a cue to continue.

"No doubt you're wondering how Leon knew so much about Krongard. The answer is simple; he's been feeding Krongard just enough information to keep him pacified. Once we realized the attention we were likely to get, we had Leon contact Krongard. Fortunately for us, not everyone is motivated by money."

"Money?" I almost asked, but Don was speaking again.

"Leon's been very valuable."

Leon's smile looked like a combination of "I did good" and "you did bad."

I was still silent, not knowing where to begin, what to say. For that matter, whatever I said now would be a waste of time. Leon still wore his half smirk, but Don's face just held disappointment, as though he had just caught his favorite student cheating on a test. Close. So rather than say anything, I just slumped in my chair.

"You'll stay here in the complex until we're finished with the project," Don continued. "Leon is submitting fake progress reports to Krongard, and we can't afford for them to be contradicted."

So at least they didn't know I had managed to use an outside communication line. Realizing that they weren't omniscient made me feel slightly better.

"If you were so distrustful of me, weren't you afraid I might just take the prototype out directly, without ever taking it to Leon?" I asked finally.

"Not at all. Those boards are useless." Leon spoke for the first time since Don had come in. "Not only didn't they perform any vital function, they didn't even work. They were just handy rejects."

"Pat said a lot about you," Don said, preparing to leave. "I really didn't expect this from you, but we had to know where your loyalties lie. I still can't believe that you'd resort to violence, so you won't be confined." He took one last, long look at me, as though examining an oddity, and then they both left.

I sat for several minutes, sorting out all the new information. Fighting the urge to chase after them and explain my actions, I became more and more convinced that their minds were made up and nothing I could say would change them. I would have told them more, but there was no way to prove it.

I could imagine what Lisa would think of the whole fiasco, but maybe Pat would talk to me. I suddenly felt lonelier than I had in years. Here I was in limbo. I couldn't get out of the complex and simply go about my life, and I was barred from the group inside.

I was ready to go find Pat and try to talk to her when the chime on my room terminal sounded, indicating an incoming message. I wasn't expecting anything. Maybe, I thought, it's Pat telling me she doesn't even want to *see* me.

It wasn't from Pat. At least I assumed not. The note was anonymous, in a sense. The message was brief: KRONGARD WILL NOT BE PLEASED THAT YOU FELL FOR THEIR SETUP, BUT AT LEAST YOU CAN BE TRUSTED. BE MORE CAREFUL WHEN YOU ARE WORKING WITH ME. I WILL CONTACT YOU LATER. NORTH STAR Q.

So there *was* an infiltrator inside the complex. Unless this was still another test from Don. But no, he couldn't have any doubts now.

North Star Q. The name didn't reveal anything. It was just a blind-drop box name in that context, which meant that I could reply to the same name and the message would get to whoever sent me the message. There was, unfortunately, no way to trace it.

Blind-drop names were one of the concessions made to the Rights for Privacy Committee. Boxes worked only in local-node areas, but within an area like this complex anyone had access to them. If I sent a message back to North Star, anyone in the local node could theoretically get access to it. But first they had to know the name North Star Q. The complication was that there was no capability to catalog all of the currently used boxes, which meant that either you knew the name or you were out of luck.

To keep the system uncluttered, all box messages were deleted at local midnight, whether or not they had been accessed after being generated. In addition, anyone who knew the name could delete the message, before or after reading it. To negate the bright idea of having a thousand monkeys all typing on their little terminals, or writing a computer program that would try every com-

bination of letters, the system employed an additional
precaution.

After each request for a box name, if it existed or not,
the system locked that user out for five seconds. It
wasn't a terribly long time, but it was long enough to
guarantee that no one terminal could make more than
17,280 requests in one day. And that was a small enough
number to keep the system honest.

So I could communicate with North Star without
anyone intercepting the message. But did I want to?

After several minutes of thought, I switched on my
room terminal and entered the message WHENEVER YOU
SAY, and transmitted it to box North Star Q.

As always, each step further into the mire brought
with it more questions. What was North Star planning
to do? Who was North Star? For all I knew, it could be
Lisa or even Pat. No. I *knew* Pat. And Lisa, in spite of
all of her shell games, still seemed particularly ill-suited
to deception. She was certainly as capable as anyone of
keeping a secret, but there was no way that I could envi-
sion her in a role of betrayal.

Could Leon be doing a triple-cross, merely helping
identify me in order to strengthen his own position? If
he was, why then wouldn't he warn me, so I knew what
to expect?

I quit speculating. It could even be Don, or it could be
any one of dozens of people I had never met, maybe
never even seen.

I still wanted to talk to Pat, but she was probably in
bed by now, so I sent her a brief note with the priority
high enough that she'd see it in the morning, but low
enough that it wouldn't wake her. I went to bed exhausted and didn't set my alarm.

I slept fitfully at first, but I didn't wake up until after

1000. Sitting on the side of the bed, trying to shrug off the drowsiness, I realized that Pat hadn't heeded my note. I had asked her to stop by my room on her way to breakfast.

The mess hall was deserted when I arrived. Thankfully, the dispensers weren't quite empty. I was hungrier than I first realized. The food satisfied my appetite, but I was no closer to talking with Pat.

Actually I most wanted to talk to Lisa, but it wouldn't be very surprising if she didn't share that desire. Lacking any alternative plans, I waited in the mess hall for Pat. She would get there eventually.

She arrived at about 1215, and not a moment too soon. Already it was apparent that the word was out: Mike Cavantalo isn't one of us. The only communications from people arriving before her had been limited to deep scowls. No one came over and threatened me, but neither did anyone talk to me.

Pat was no different. I tried to get her to sit at my table and talk for a few minutes. I couldn't even persuade her to say one word. Her penetrating gaze, filled with anger and shame, said it all. I felt a little like Ebenezer Scrooge might feel during a vision, trying to say or do something that could change the course of even the next minute and failing.

Even more demoralized than before, I left the mess hall before Lisa could arrive. That was all I needed, to get the same treatment from her and Pat, all in the same ten minutes. I was tense, nervous. Walking seemed like one way to burn off the energy and calm down, so I did. I walked and walked. A couple of hours later my physical energy had abated, but my thoughts and feelings were still accelerated.

Imagining a scene with Lisa, similar to the one with Pat, I decided to see Lisa in her room rather than in the mess hall. At least there wouldn't be any peer pressure on her to ostracize me. If she did, it would be because that was the way she felt.

Seeing her in her quarters necessitated a wait until the evening. About to set an alarm to remind me, I realized how foolish that was. I wouldn't forget it. I wouldn't even stop thinking about it. I had to talk to someone and I wanted Lisa to be that person.

Unwilling to face the cold stares in the mess hall during dinner, I went early and grabbed a couple of sandwiches and a drink for later. I spent more time walking around the complex. There were only a few people in the corridors, and they all gave me the same treatment that the people during lunch had. Depressed, I went back to my room and ate my sandwiches.

It was finally late enough for Lisa to be back in her room, so I went there. I knocked on her door, softly to avoid other attention.

"Who is it?" she called, without opening the door. That was the first bad sign. Before, she had simply opened the door to find out who was there.

"It's me—Mike."

Silence.

After a longer delay, I tried again. "Lisa, please open the door. I need to talk to you—just for a few minutes."

More silence.

I trudged back to my room. At least I didn't have to see the expression on her face. Pat's had been devastating enough.

I was totally depressed and surprised all at the same time. I had known Lisa only a short time, but I found that her rejection hurt even worse than Pat's had. I'd been struggling to maintain my distance and objectivity, but I was beginning to realize that I might not be doing such a good job. Maybe the most recent crisis always seems to be the worst, but I felt more depressed now than I had for a long time.

Fortunately I didn't have much time to think about Lisa. There was another message from North Star waiting for me at my room terminal when I got back. Whoever it was could have sent a message to my wristcomp to tell me, but must have had some reason for not doing so. It probably wouldn't be too subtle to have someone who's being ostracized receiving messages in public.

The message was even shorter than the first one. It read: DO YOU HAVE ANY WEAPONS? Did I have any weapons? After being searched the way I had been on the way in? I almost replied, "Yes. A cunning mind and a sharp tongue," but instead transmitted, NO.

A half hour later there had still been no other response, but the longer I thought about the question, the more I worried. It was time to take stronger action.

By 0200 I had written two programs, one for my room terminal, and one for my wristcomp. The room terminal would now forward all messages to my wristcomp as they came in. Additionally it would periodically query the North Star blind-drop box. My wristcomp was now set up to suppress the beep of an incoming call if the transmission was a specially formated message, and I had that feature enabled. Now I'd be able to get North Star's messages without being in my room and without notifying anyone I happened to be near. I'd just have to check my wristcomp periodically to see if anything had come in.

The next task would be harder. I was still wide-awake, but tired, so I forced myself to get some sleep. Another sandwich from the mess hall made a barely tolerable breakfast late the next morning.

Back in my room I resumed work. The first step was

to alter and disguise my voice during a wristcomp call. I settled on a combination of two approaches.

First I programmed my wristcomp to record and scan the transmit portions of its communications, but not actually to transmit in real time. By detecting the dead space between words, it could determine the beginning and ending time of each word I spoke. Once it determined that I had finished a word, it would replay that word slightly faster, about a half octave higher in pitch, and transmit it then.

The second step was easier. I programmed a varied selection of semirandom noise to be mixed with my voice when I spoke. Some of the noise would ride the top of the signal, so when the noise was loud, the whole transmission would be loud. The remainder I used to modulate my voice, so it would fade in and out, independent of the other noise.

I could have written a program for my room terminal to let me transmit a message to it and then replay it, but fortunately it already had the capability in its diagnostic repertoire. Six tries for some fine tuning were enough to satisfy me. I had cut down the noise from my original estimate. As it was now, my voice sounded marginally understandable but hard to recognize.

My precautions might have been overdone, but I preferred to err on the side of caution this time. I was ready for the next step.

I took a deep breath and keyed in a call to Don, disabling the video. I hoped that it would work. There would be only one chance. I turned on the recorder.

"Hello," came his voice as he answered the call.

"Who's there?" I asked, holding my throat to further disguise my voice.

"It's Don," he replied with curiosity in his voice.

"Sorry." I disconnected.

It had worked, so far. I just hoped that he wouldn't get too suspicious. Wrong numbers were rare, but he shouldn't have been able to tell that it was me. Even if he could, though, it wouldn't necessarily be a disaster. He wouldn't know why.

Everything was ready. The recording sounded fine. The rest of the day passed slowly, but I felt better than I had the night before. At least I was doing something constructive.

I went to Lisa's room almost an hour earlier than I had last night, partly because she might suspect that it was me if I came at the same time, and partly because I couldn't wait any longer.

I knocked three times, slow and equally spaced, so it wouldn't sound like my regular knock. There was silence. For a moment I worried that she might not be there, but then she responded.

"Who is it?" she called, still not opening the door.

"It's Don," said my wristcomp recorder, turned up almost as loud as it could be without heavy distortion.

My heart quickened again. I was afraid she would ask why he would be there or some other question that I didn't have a recorded reply for. She didn't. The door started to swing open. As it opened wide enough for our eyes to meet, and as surprise reached her eyes, I jammed my foot into the opening.

Intent as I was on getting in, I was startled to see that her eyes were red, as though from crying.

In that same instant, hurt and anger flashed across her face, and she started to force the door closed. I had two advantages, however: surprise and weight. I came there knowing what I wanted to do, and now my body was acting almost automatically. Lisa, on the other hand, was probably shocked to realize that someone was trying to force his way into her room. Adding that advantage to my extra twenty-five kilos made the struggle fairly short.

"Lisa," I said as I found leverage between the door and the wall. "I've got to talk to you."

Her physical resistance faded, whether because of my comment or the fact that she knew she couldn't prevent it, I didn't know. And then I was inside. I pushed the door closed and locked it.

Lisa wouldn't meet my gaze. She turned away and then sat on her bed, her back expressing her feelings.

"Lisa, I'm sorry. I didn't want to do this—force my way in—but I had to talk to you."

She didn't respond.

"Look. There are some things that I have to explain to you. When I'm done, I'll leave you alone permanently, if that's what you want."

Still no response.

"Can we talk for just a couple of minutes?" I asked. She remained silent. As I stood there, wondering what to do next, I saw a faint trembling in her shoulders and head.

"Lisa?" I said, approaching her. I put my hand on her shoulder, touching her for the first time, but she drew away. She was crying.

I felt rotten. Here was one person to whom I didn't want anything to happen. I didn't even like the idea of her being sad. Yet I was the one who was the cause of it all. Worried for a moment that I might make matters even worse by staying, I almost left. But I couldn't.

I sat on the bed beside her and tried to put my arm around her. She shrugged it off. Not knowing what else to do, I took off my wristcomp and punched a few keys so the display that I had generated earlier came up on its screen. I would have sent her a message if there hadn't been the possibility of a tap.

"Lisa," I said softly. "I'll leave in one minute if you want me to. But first I want you to read this. Please." I touched my wristcomp to her arm so she would know what it was.

She was still for a long moment before she slowly moved to wipe her eyes. Without looking at me, she grasped my wristcomp and held it so she could see it.

The letters weren't visible from my angle, but I knew what they said: I DID NOT BETRAY YOUR GROUP. BEFORE I TURNED OVER THE PROTOTYPE AND NOTES, I DAMAGED THEM TO MAKE THEM UNUSABLE.

chapter
SIXTEEN

Lisa slowly turned around to look at me after she finished reading the message on my wristcomp. The defiance in her eyes gradually gave way to questioning and surprise.

She drew a breath, but before she could speak, I raised a finger to my lips to keep her quiet. Taking my wristcomp from her hands, I punched another couple of buttons and brought up a display of another canned message that I had stored.

This time the words read: YOUR ROOM MAY BE BUGGED. THERE ARE OTHER THINGS I MUST TALK TO YOU ABOUT. ARE YOU WILLING TO MEET ME AND TALK?

After she read the second message her eyes met mine. I hoped that she could see from my eyes that I was telling her the truth. After a hesitation she nodded. I smiled a lips-together grin to say thanks.

My last wristcomp message asked her to meet me in an unused room on the second floor of the next building. It would be relatively secure, but not so far off the heavily used path that it would create suspicion if we

were seen individually. Another nod indicated her
agreement. She wiped her eyes before rising to leave, apparently conscious of the reddening and puffiness.

Preparations complete, I said, "Well, if you're not
willing to talk, I'll leave you alone." I winked and
tapped my ear.

Lisa went out first and signaled that the hall was
clear. I closed the door behind me rapidly and moved
down the hall in the direction opposite the one she took.
I didn't want anyone to see us together.

I took a circuitous path to the room where we were
to meet. She probably beat me there by four or five minutes. I entered and locked the door behind me quietly.
Lisa was sitting on a stack of musty old shipping crates.

I was trying to figure out where to begin when she
spoke.

"Is what you showed me really true?" The storeroom
lighting gave her darker eyes, making her look even sad-
der.

"Yes." I sat on a box near her.

She looked at me for a long time. When she finally
looked away, I was able to gather enough concentration
to start explaining.

"First of all, it's true that I was sent here by Krongard. Wait, just hear me out, okay?" I said as she
started to rise. "The details aren't too important any
longer, but he blackmailed me into coming. I didn't tell
anyone because I wanted to stay here, and I didn't want
him to know that I didn't intend to cooperate."

Lisa relaxed a bit as I continued.

"I didn't know what to do when Leon approached me
with the idea of stealing the prototype. I didn't want to
betray the group and I didn't want Krongard to know
that I wasn't following the plan. I'd still like to be able
to get another job when this is all over.

"So I decided to damage the board and notes so they wouldn't be usable by Krongard. I was pretty sure that I could stick them both in an oven—one of the process-control ovens—but I didn't know how hot or how long. I wanted to guarantee that they were damaged but not melted. A friend of mine looked up the figures for me."

"What? How did you—" she started.

"I snuck into the third-floor area and used the main-net link."

"You're absolutely *sure* you don't do this for a living?"

"Yes. Anyway, the notes were heated up enough to scatter the crystals totally. They won't be legible *or* reconstructable.   The prototype was harder. I heated it up enough to lower the transmission efficiency of all of the fiber-optic interconnections. The right amount of heat makes them very slightly opaque. Now their efficiency is less than a tenth of a percent of normal. The board looks fine, but it won't work worth a damn."

"But why didn't you tell them that when you realized it was a test?"

"At first I couldn't believe what was happening to me, and by the time I did, they told me that the board was trash. It never worked in the first place. So how could I convince them that I had subtly damaged it?"

She didn't reply to the rhetorical question, so I continued. "Lisa, do you believe me? I've had a lot of time lately to think, and I've realized it's very important to me that you believe me."

"Why is that?" Her voice was unsteady and huskier than normal.

I looked at her, but she was still staring into the shadows on the far side of the room. "Several reasons," I said. "One of which is that I'm more attracted to you than any woman I've met in a long time."

Our eyes met and locked on each other's.

"I think I do believe you," she said in a whisper-soft voice.

I felt so much better I almost forgot the rest of what I had to tell her.

"Now for the bad news," I said with a levity I didn't really feel. "Unless you're still testing me, there really is a spy in here."

At first she didn't realize that I was serious. Then I explained about the messages from North Star. She rubbed her hands together as I talked.

"And I don't know what the plan is, not even the next step," I concluded.

"So that's why you were afraid that my room might have been wired for sound," she said at last, evidently recovering.

"Yes. It hasn't taken much recently to trigger my paranoia. Maybe I'm a latent paranoid. I don't know. I can't imagine that every room in the complex is bugged, but it's easy to believe that some of the most frequently used ones are."

"And that's why you couldn't send me a message— it might be intercepted," she said, tapping her palm against her forehead. "Things are beginning to fall into place."

I, too, could notice the change. Earlier that night Lisa had been lethargic and seemingly slow to comprehend. Now she was functioning more normally, her quick mind again fitting the facts together and deducing the missing portions of the picture.

"Lisa," I started tentatively. "Why were you—" I stopped.

"Go on," she urged.

"Why the crying earlier? What was wrong?"

"You have to ask?" She paused. "I thought you were smarter than that." Her smile swept away the sting in the words. "I've really enjoyed myself with you. The idea that you had been sent here to do a job and—and tell whatever lies you had to in the process—" She faltered.

I reached out and took her hand. I don't know what I had intended to say, but I forgot whatever it was when I looked into her eyes again. This time there was a quality in them that I hadn't seen before. Lisa, rather than looking strong and intelligent right then, looked alone.

The next thing I knew, we were in each other's arms. After a while I realized that I might be hurting her, so I relaxed my grip. Somehow holding Lisa seemed strange and natural at the same time.

"I'm on your side," I said a little later. "I didn't mean for you to be hurt by all of this."

In answer she held tighter.

I could have stayed there all night, but if anyone was looking for Lisa, it would probably create suspicion in at least one person's mind. "Lisa, there are a couple more things I have to talk about before we go back," I said, gently pulling away.

"All right."

"For one thing, I don't think you should tell anyone about the infiltrator."

"You make 'anyone' sound all-inclusive."

"I think it should be. Don himself could be playing both sides for all I know. I can't believe that it's you or Pat. I'm afraid my seeing her would be more likely to cause suspicion, though."

"Is that why you came to see me?" she asked, a trace of disappointment in her voice.

"No. I came to see you because I didn't want you thinking what everyone else is thinking about me— because I wanted to see you."

"Thanks."

"I don't think you should tell even Pat. The more

people who know, the more who are going to have to *act* angry at me. And we run the risk of telling the infiltrator. It's just you and me. But if you get to feeling suspicious of me, check out that prototype board. You can tell that it's been damaged when you know what to look for.''

"I can't. It was thrown away. It wasn't useful in the first place; that's why it was used. But it doesn't matter. I believe you.''

We had been there long enough for me to start worrying about her absence being detected, but I wasn't finished.

"We'd better arrange for communications. I think we'd be safer using a blind-drop box. Do you want to choose a name?''

"How aobut 'Tennis Elbow'?''

"Fine. Stick out your wristcomp. I've got a program for you." I beamed over to her wristcomp my program that would run on her room terminal and send a message to her wristcomp if it found any activity in a blind-drop box. I explained what it would do. "The only item it prompts you for is a list of blind-drop file names to scan.''

"Okay.''

"One more thing," I said, stirring uncomfortably on the crate I had chosen for a seat. "I don't want to worry you, but I want to be honest with you.''

"Go on," Lisa urged after I hesitated.

"I'm trying to figure out how to explain it. I've got this conflict—between wanting to help you, and not liking what you're doing. At this point I'm not too happy about what anybody's doing. But I want you to know that my loyalties are with you and Pat and the group.''

"What do you mean, you don't like what we're doing?''

"I mean I've had a lot of time to think lately, and I

don't feel comfortable with the idea of a long-range scapescope. As a matter of fact, I'm not sure I even like the idea of the regular scapescope." I stopped, expecting her to be defending her goals, but she was very quiet.

"Lisa, I'm not saying that I won't help. Don't worry about that."

"What don't you like about the long-range scapescope?" She wouldn't look at me now.

"I'm not sure I even know all the reasons. Mainly, I guess, I don't know that it's good for us. We've had scapescopes for quite a few years now, and I'm beginning to think they're not really helping us. But I don't want to start an argument right now. I respect your beliefs, and I don't intend to help Krongard. Can we leave it at that?"

"Mike, I—oh, all right."

"Okay. We'd better get back. I don't want to advertise the fact that I saw you. You won't tell anyone?"

In answer Lisa crossed her heart and grinned, her green eyes soft and happy. Either she believed me or she was one truly fine actress. She made me feel great. A compassionate woman is proof that beauty is *not* only skin-deep.

"How about if I leave first?" Lisa suggested. "If the hall is empty, I'll knock on the door."

"Fine. I'll probably wait at least five minutes before I go anyway."

She paused, about to open the door. "Mike, I'll have to treat you like before."

"Yeah. I know. I can stand it for a while since I know it won't be real." I put my hand on hers. "And thanks for believing me."

"I wanted to." Lisa gave my hand a quick squeeze, and then she was gone.

A moment later a quick knock told me that the corridor was clear, but I waited ten more minutes to play safe. At the end of my wait I slowly opened the door until there was a one-centimeter gap. Except for the gentle *whoosh* of the air circulation, not a sound reached my ears for the next couple of minutes, so I left and took the long way back to my room. The journey went without incident.

I slept better that night than I had in weeks. Breakfast the next morning put a strain on me, though. I woke up at my usual time and struggled down to the mess hall to eat. As it turned out, Lisa and Pat were both there already.

They ignored me, of course. In spite of knowing that Lisa was acting and Pat would likely believe me if I told her, it still bothered me. In a way akin to the feelings I got when someone described a grisly crime, even though I wasn't the victim, I felt uncomfortable. Maybe it was too easy for me to visualize the same thing happening to me or, in this case, Lisa getting angry at me and snubbing me for real. Her acting was realistic, if anything. I resolved to continue eating at times other than regular mealtimes.

It might have helped to send a note to Lisa via the blind-drop box, but I decided that I didn't feel comfortable doing so, and I wasn't sure what to say anyway.

I dropped back into a routine of walking randomly through the complex. Until I heard from my unknown cohort, there wasn't much I could do. Two more uneventful days passed, and then another message arrived from North Star.

The message read: I HAVE A JOB FOR YOU. AFTER 2000 TONIGHT FIND A BROWN PACKAGE IN ROOM 1662 BEHIND THE TOP PANEL IN THE EQUIPMENT RACK. TAKE THE PACKAGE AND LEAVE IT CONCEALED IN THE LOCAL-NODE COMPUTER ROOM. DO NOT DROP IT.

There was plenty of time before 2000 to ponder the

message, but nothing came to mind that could calm the initial surge of nervousness that sprang into me when I read the words, "Do not drop it." Those words ruled out the possibility of a simple communications disruptor. I wasn't very pleased with the idea of carrying around a package that contained enough power to damage the contents of a whole room, but that was the only easy explanation. Unless it was another test, in which case it didn't matter anyway. No. This had the feel of the real thing.

The building maps showed me where the local-node computer room was. As was true of most places in the complex, there were more than two ways to get there. Several of them would take me through high-traffic areas, so the choice was easy.

I preferred to go as late as possible, to lessen the chances of being seen. However, there could have easily been a timer set to detonate the package after a reasonable delay—or an unreasonable delay. Having it explode while I was carrying it in my pocket sounded particularly unpleasant. And I'd probably get really strange looks from anyone seeing me dragging a package behind me on a ten-meter cord. I left promptly at 2000.

The package was easy to find. It was in an old equipment rack, just where North Star said it would be. Judging from the thickness of the dust on the components inside, the rack had been a pretty good hiding place.

The package was small, about three by five centimeters on the sides and less than a centimeter thick. A brown wrapper kept its contents from being inspected. I carried it slightly away from my body. If it really was an explosive, I was probably as safe as I would be running as fast as I could from a star that would go nova in the next minute.

I almost made it out of the heavily traveled area with-

out problem. I was nearly at a T intersection of two corridors when I heard voices. They were growing louder. I
really didn't want to be caught with what was probably
a bomb. Whoever found me now might be tempted
simply to lock me and the package in a room and go
away for a long time.

There was no time to retreat and hide. I could only
hope that they weren't going to come down the hall I
was in. A structural steel beam could conceal me from
their view if they kept going straight, so I hid behind it.

I could hear their voices more clearly now, but I
didn't recognize them. Belatedly I wondered if maybe I
should have bluffed my way through. If they found me
here, obviously hiding, it was all over. The real infiltrator would be free to do whatever he wanted, and I'd be
locked up for sure.

I understood then why the infiltrator wanted me to be
doing this job. If I were caught, nothing new would
be learned. But if he were discovered, there wouldn't be
anyone left to do Krongard's dirty work.

My throat constricted suddenly as I heard voices that
sounded as if they were coming from less than a meter
away, but no one saw me. They continued along the
main corridor. Evidently the sound had bounced off a
couple of metallic walls.

The sound of footsteps faded slowly, and my breathing relaxed. I edged cautiously to the intersection and
looked first one way and then the other. The two
strollers had just turned the far corner, so I took the
corridor in the opposite direction. The stairwell at the
next intersection led up to the third floor, to an area that
was much less likely to be traveled.

Some of my tension dissipated as I climbed the stairs.
I had looked at the map long enough earlier to feel fairly
confident about which way to go next, but the hard

copy I unfolded made me feel better. A right turn at the next corner intersection revealed another long corridor. At sporadic intervals defective light panels left sections of the hallway in semidarkness. The combined effect of the dark panels and my frame of mind gave the passage a spooky quality. It reminded me of old pictures of auto highways—night scenes that showed a dark road partially illuminated by overhead lights spaced at overlong intervals.

Now more than at any previous time I was acutely aware of the age of the complex. At home failures were corrected within minutes. This corridor might not have received attention for fifty years. In the heavily used areas of the mountain complex, someone was still replacing defective components. But not here. It was dark enough that the solar cells on my compband probably wouldn't be able to keep my wristcomp charged if I stayed in the area for a month or more.

I quickened my pace. This section of the complex made me feel isolated, as if I were out in the country, far away from people and buildings. The feeling was different from the feeling I got in a park. There, even though I might be out of sight of another person for a little while, there was always someone close. Right now I was ambivalent about the idea of seeing another person.

I reached the next intersection. Here I had to take a right, down a short hall, before reaching my destination, but now the corridor was almost completely black. I took it slowly, with my arms outstretched, but I still bumped into an old fire extinguisher. My ego was doing better until I speeded up slightly and tripped over an obstruction.

There wasn't anything actually lying on the floor. The floor was raised. For reasons perhaps known only to a long-dead, maniacal plumber or electrician, the floor level rose twenty to thirty centimeters and dropped back down after a short interval.

At the end of the darkened area I could see better, and I finally found the door that must lead to the local-node computer room. It was unlocked. Stepping into the room was reassuring. This area was much brighter, with all but a few of the light panels still in operation. I locked the door behind me.

The room held more equipment than any room I had been in except the lab, but most of it looked obsolete. The far wall was lined with equipment racks, mostly filled with equipment so old that it used electrical cables for interconnections. Out of the expanse of racks, there was one cabinet whose panels sported mil-standard fiber-optic cable connectors. Someone must have upgraded the normal functions of this room long ago and left the original system as a backup—or left it because it was too much trouble to remove. The single rack was either the replacement system or perhaps a system brought in by the group.

I couldn't see any other modern equipment in the room, so that rack must be the only place to avoid when hiding the package. Probably no one visited this room very often, but if someone did, the new equipment wouldn't be a good hiding place.

In the far corner a grimy assortment of rack-mounted equipment with finger-twist fastenings appeared to be a good hiding place. I loosened one of the eye-level panels and pulled myself up a few centimeters to see inside. Perfect. The unit that slid out from the rack was an indicator panel and behind it was mostly unused space, plenty of room for the package.

So close to completing the job, I finally let my curiosity run rampant. Maybe I shouldn't have opened the package. For all I knew, it might have been set to explode on opening. But the wrapping looked like regular shrinkwrap, so I decided to go ahead.

A kneeling position on the floor wasn't comfortable, but it was about the easiest way. I slowly pulled at the top corner and it gradually lengthened, exposing the material inside, a dull-red, pasty substance. I exposed more and stopped to stare.

No one trusted me. Even this crazy North Star person. Now revealed were two beads that looked like map pins stuck into the red substance, and one of them had the color markings of a transponder. So all North Star had to do was walk around the complex with a small transceiver and he could find the package. It would sit here quietly until it received a message meant for it, and then it would retransmit it in a short burst. North Star could triangulate it, maybe not getting any nearer than a few hundred meters, depending on the signal strength and the construction of the walls. Certainly if he came here, he could find it quickly or know that I didn't bring it.

Was this another test? Did North Star not trust me, or was he just plain thorough? Maybe he wanted to move it again after I left it here. No. That explanation didn't make sense. I didn't know why he wanted it in this room or even how he got it into the complex, but I was convinced that it was an explosive.

Then what was the other bead? I couldn't tell, but it could conceivably be either a receiver detonator or a countdown-clock detonator, or both. So, if I was daring —no, make that foolhardy—I could maybe pull the bead off and thereby defuse the device. Even assuming that in the process I didn't make a mistake that would turn my body into a new coat of paint on the walls, it wouldn't work. All North Star had to do was double-check on me and I might end up in the same condition anyway.

I couldn't think of any other alternatives, so I released the shrinkwrap and watched while it slowly contracted until once again it formed a smooth, form-fitting covering. The recurring idea that the second bead might be a receiver or timer detonator hastened my movements, and I gently placed the package into the equipment rack. The panel slid shut smoothly. I filed its location away in that voluminous portion of my brain that vividly remembers information that has an almost unbelievably small need to be recalled.

I started back to my quarters, realizing that the idea of being separated into many pieces had overshadowed my fears of being unpleasantly surprised by one of the group members. The latter was no longer much of a threat. Without the package there was nothing to indicate that I wasn't simply out for a walk, albeit in an out-of-the-way place. Of course, that might change if I was seen this close to the computer room and it was mysteriously destroyed soon after.

My trip had taken longer than I expected. I made it all the way back to my room without seeing another person—or hearing or feeling an explosion. My obligatory message to North Star was brief: DONE, NOW WHAT? I waited awhile for a response, but nothing was forthcoming.

By the time I made up my mind that I wanted to talk to Lisa, it was so late that she was surely asleep. Any box message I sent her wouldn't be there when she woke up since they were all deleted at midnight, but I sent one anyway, just in case. It was short since I expected to type a longer one in the morning. The message read: DON'T GO NEAR THE LOCAL-NODE COMPUTER ROOM. SIGNED, A SECRET ADMIRER.

I was getting ready for bed when my room terminal beeped. Lisa had been awake. Her reply said simply: WHY?

My spirits lifted a bit and I reached over and typed: IF I TELL YOU, IT WON'T BE A SECRET ANYMORE.

NO. WHY DON'T GO NEAR?

THE ROOM NOW HAS A RESIDENT BOMB, I THINK.

TELL ME MORE.

I had typed in several sentences when I changed my mind and typed instead: LET'S MEET.

HOW ABOUT IN RIO?

HOW ABOUT THE SAME PLACE AS LAST TIME?

IT WILL HAVE TO DO. FIFTEEN MINUTES?

ROGER, WILCO.

YOU MEAN YES?

YES.

I was the first one there, but Lisa kept me waiting for only a minute or two.

"What's all this about a bomb?" she asked after she closed the door. I was already perched on a shipping crate.

"I'm pretty sure that's what it is," I said, and went on to describe the rest of my adventure.

"Okay, but why?" she asked as I finished.

"Why put the bomb there, or why me?"

"Both."

"In reverse order, my best guess is that whoever it is can't afford to be caught skulking around at funny times or locations. As for the other, I don't know, but it seems that things are about to start happening soon. How close are you to having your new scapescope done? Once it's working and you get plans distributed to other locations, that will reduce the pressure here."

Lisa didn't answer immediately. At first I worried that she might still not trust me, but that doubt was obliterated by her next words.

"We'll probably be ready to try it out by tomorrow night or, at the latest, the day after," she said, and then turned back to face me. "But there's more. I was afraid to tell you earlier, but we're not working on a long-range scapescope. We want to *eliminate* scapescope."

chapter
SEVENTEEN

"You're working to *eliminate* scapescope?" I asked. After a moment's reflection, I added, "That's terrific! How?" Lisa's admission had my thoughts racing again. Of course. That's why they didn't want the government to know. And that explained the cover story they must have "accidentally" leaked out—a long-range scapescope was probably a great idea as far as Krongard was concerned.

"That's really not my area, but I can give you an outsider's view, if you want," Lisa replied.

"Go ahead."

"The easiest way I've heard it explained is by analogy to a pond of water. The Newbury-Kalmez field is the water. We can see through it with the assistance of scapescope. Currents started in the water are like noise in the field; they stir up mud and silt at the bottom of the pond and make visibility poorer."

"So you're going to stir up the mud?"

"Basically. But we have to be careful. Just like in a real ecosystem, say the pond, there are a lot of vari-

189

ables. What we want to do is turn on a transmitter long enough to cause portions of the field to start harmonic oscillations. Time waves, if you will. That *should* create enough noise in the field to leave it unusable for, we hope, fifty years or so. Maybe by then we'll have thought more about the problems scapescope is causing. That's how long it should take for the oscillations to die out."

"So this will happen tomorrow night?"

"That's the plan, but we've still got some last-minute problems to work out. Even after all the time we've known about the field, there are still a lot of puzzles. Who knows? If our theories are wrong, we could wind up polarizing the field, or creating enough disturbance to last a week, or creating only enough noise to last the length of time that the transmitter is turned on. If that happened, then we'd have the problem of trying to protect the transmitter from Brother Sammy."

"Well, if it's going to work, wouldn't that mean that on all the government scapescopes they can't see past tomorrow? It seems like they'd be breaking down the doors to get in here."

"No. The device starts a reaction that takes several months or more to reach equilibrium. During that time the visibility through the field should slowly drop from six months to nothing. Once the disruptor is turned on, if it works, they won't be able to do anything, and they won't get any advance warning."

"But can't they build a device of their own that would counteract the effects of yours?"

"Maybe, given enough time. And maybe not. I don't know. Even if they do, probably we'll have learned a little bit more by then."

I suddenly felt much better. I had resolved to help the group in spite of my feelings, but Lisa's revelation sure made it easier. "I'm glad you told me all this," I said. "Scapescope bothers me even more than I told you."

"Why?"

"For one thing, knowing that something bad is going to happen, but being unable to change it, simply has to be one of the most frustrating problems a person can have to deal with." Lisa raised her eyebrows but didn't interrupt. "And knowing that something good is going to happen takes away some sense of pride in accomplishment. Maybe it's turning us into a near-sighted culture, looking only a few months into the future. There's more, but I guess that's enough."

"One of the side effects that bothers us most," Lisa said when I paused, "is that we're discouraging talents that the human race won't outgrow the need for. We're punishing persistence and endurance. Before scapescope if, say, a scientist or a politician started out poorly, that might have been the end of a project or a career. But then again, that person might have decided that the goal was worth the emotional investment and would struggle longer. Now someone in the same position is given no choice. Either the funding for a project is cut because there are no immediate, visible results, or people don't vote for the politician who doesn't have reasonably good chances to win the first time. By penalizing persistence, we're turning people into drones who understand only instant gratification."

I hadn't thought of it quite that way, but I could suddenly see those qualities in my old job. And I could see that the focus of my own efforts had been on economics and production efficiency at the expense of innovation.

"My job—" I said. "I probably won't have much of a job when this is all over." Even if Krongard were willing.

"You'll survive. You're intelligent. There will be a lot

of changes rippling down from this, but people will work things out. Particularly if they know that they have to. They always have.''

''I hope you're right.''

''By the way, have you been eating lately?'' Lisa asked, exercising her occasional talent for right-angle turns in the topic of conversation.

''Sure, why—oh. Yeah, I've been eating, but I haven't been going at regular mealtimes. Sometimes the—ah—social pressure gets to me.''

''You mean the ostracism? They'll change once this is over and we can tell them.''

''I don't care about the others. It's like that old saying, 'You always hurt the one you love.' I think what that really means is that you can't be hurt by anyone you don't care about. I don't care about the feelings of people I don't know. They don't mean anything to me. But when you and Pat ignore me in there, no matter how many times I tell myself that you're acting and she's uninformed, it still bothers me. Maybe my subconscious thinks that Pat should have accepted on faith the fact that I wouldn't betray her.''

''I wish I could do something. I think I understand some of what you feel.''

''I thought you might. What's happened to you, Lisa? You're bright, enthusiastic, pretty—but you hold it all in.''

''It's not something I feel comfortable talking about yet.'' She shifted her gaze and looked back into the shadows. ''The capsule summary is that I spent quite a while with someone I loved, and made major sacrifices for, and it ended. I don't want that to happen ever again.'' Her eyes grew cold as she spoke.

''I wish there was something I could do.''

''Maybe you can. I see things in your eyes that I never saw in his.''

"Like what?"

Lisa's hands formed a T for time-out. "I just need some time. There's too much going on right now, okay?"

"Okay, Lisa. I don't mean to push. I just want to know you better. I'll drop the subject for now."

Her expression softened, and she gave me a mild grin. I didn't want to leave, but the longer we were gone, the greater chance there was of our simultaneous absences being noticed. Lisa left first again. Long afterward I could still see the wink she had given me when she left. It made me feel grateful that I was strong enough to survive but not so strong that I didn't need other people. Some people seemed to want guarantees on how things would work out. Others apparently accepted good odds. I hoped that Lisa fit into the good-odds category.

The following morning I woke up starving, but I still waited until the mess hall should have been unoccupied. It was. As I sat there, warming my hands on a hot mug, my recent conversations with Lisa seemed like dream sequences. She had said that there was too much going on, and she was right. I felt as though my mind had been living at a sedate pace for so long that it was still running a few days or weeks behind.

With no one to talk with, I found that the rest of the day seemed interminable. My only sense of accomplishment was that at least I ate well. At that moment it didn't give me any pride, but at breakfast I didn't realize how much energy I would need that night, and what a fine line there was between exhaustion and extinction.

I was feeling cut off from the world as I sat in my room that night. I didn't know what North Star was doing, and I had no idea what progress the group was making. Lisa had said maybe tonight.

Shortly my room terminal beeped again, with a message from Lisa. She was starting a two-hour break before going back to work. I replied, and we met a few minutes later in our regular conference room.

"We're almost there," she said as soon as she saw me. "If things go well, we'll be able to activate the disruptor within six to eight hours."

"That's a pretty narrow estimate. I'm surprised that you didn't say 'sometime in the next two days.' "

"That's because it's already built, and Celeste is reasonably certain that it will function the way it's intended to. All that's left now is to finish up some functional tests of individual components and then make final adjustments on a few of the variable parameters, like signal frequency. We're so close that no one will sleep tonight, so we voted to continue."

"Shouldn't you be resting?" I asked. It was a silly question. Lisa couldn't look much more vibrant and alert.

"No. I wanted to see you. And to find out if you've learned anything more about our unknown friend."

"Not a word. That worries me. Maybe he's planning on doing whatever it is that he's going to do by himself. With things so close to completion, he has to make his move soon. I'd better let you get back so no one notices your absence."

"Just one more thing before we go. I wanted to explain why I was—oh, aloof—the day or two before you brought the prototype to Leon. I knew about the test. So did Pat. We were both against it but couldn't prevent it. I felt rotten about the whole affair."

"Don't. You did what you had to. Let's just leave it at that."

Moments later Lisa was on her way to her room for a brief rest before the balance of the evening. I didn't go back to my room. If anything was going to happen, it would be soon, so I stayed tense.

Why didn't North Star send a message? Surely he must be up to something by now. I walked the halls, only occasionally seeing someone else out. An hour later I realized that I had seen no one for the last fifteen minutes. The late-night session must have started, which meant that, besides the guard at the door and any stragglers, the only other person who might be up and around was North Star.

I was almost prepared to start roaming corridors in outlying sections of the complex when it happened. My wristcomp beeped gently and I found a newly arrived text message.

It was from North Star, but it hadn't been sent to the blind-drop box. It was routed directly to me. So North Star wasn't worried about it being intercepted.

The message was short. If North Star had any good qualities, brevity was among them. The text read: MEET ME NOW IN ROOM 1662. NORTH STAR. I remembered the room. It was the place where I had found the package.

Several possibilities flashed through my brain. One, I could call Don and tell him where North Star was. Except that it might be another setup, and then North Star would know not to trust me. Two, I could go there and be killed because North Star had somehow found out about Lisa and the truth. Three, I could go there, meet North Star, and grab the first opportunity to disrupt his plans. The third possibility was the only one that gave me any hope.

If I'd had a secret arsenal, I would have made a quick detour to grab a laser pistol, a neuronic paralyzer, a protection vest, and a manual describing how to use them. As it was, I started moving toward the meeting place. At least I'd find out who North Star was.

The door was unlocked, but the lights were out. I was grasping for the light switch, feeling very exposed, when a voice from the darkness startled me.

"You took your time getting here." The deep, throaty quality of the voice sounded suddenly familiar.

"I came as fast as I could," I said as my fingers brushed the switch. "Leon," I added as the room flooded with light. Leon Rubotto.

"Who else?" he asked. A self-satisfied grin made him look even more sinister than his rough features already did. "There're just the two of us."

"Why didn't you tell me before?"

"No need. The less you knew, the better off I was." Did Krongard rub off on people?

"Well, why didn't you at least warn me about the setup—anonymously?"

"It was useful to me too. I needed to make sure whose side you were on. In fact, I was responsible for it. I dropped a suggestion at the right time and just sat back to watch. But we don't have time to talk."

"Why? What are you doing?"

"It's time for us to leave, and I need your help."

"Leave? Already? The project is still going on, isn't it?" I added quickly.

"That's being taken care of." Leon's voice was confident. Although he was no longer grinning openly, a suggestion of a smile still tugged at his lips.

I was afraid, for the moment, to ask exactly what he meant. "How do we get out?" I asked instead.

"We walk out the front doors." Leon looked at his wristcomp for the third time in the last minute. "In fact, the first part of the schedule is happening—now. The local-node computer is, as of this moment, disabled. They shouldn't notice that it's down unless they need it for communications. And I don't want them communicating."

I punched a couple of keys on my wristcomp to make a simple system access, and on the screen flashed a

message I had never seen before: CENTRAL COMPUTER
DOES NOT REPLY. DIAGNOSTICS INDICATE NO TRANSMIT-
TER/RECEIVER MALFUNCTION IN WRISTCOMP. REPORT
TROUBLE MANUALLY.

"Explosive?" I asked.

"Right." Leon glanced at me but didn't say anything
more.

"But I didn't feel a thing."

"It's two buildings away. Did you forget about the
shock absorbers? Besides, it was a tiny one. Come on.
We need to go." He opened the door and started off at
a brisk pace.

"How did you smuggle that in?" I asked, catching up
with him.

"I didn't. The only thing I brought in was this." He
patted a small bulge at his beltline. It had to be a pistol.
"And some extra information about the complex. The
explosives were already here. I don't know why. Maybe
they wanted a way to blast their way out if they ever got
trapped in here."

"But you smuggled in a laser pistol?"

"You can't be too careful with a nut group like this
one. And it wasn't that hard, since I was trusted. I
brought it in between the doors and left it there, one day
when I was out to get supplies. A day later, when it was
my turn for guard duty, I opened up the inside door and
grabbed the gun."

I didn't actually care how he had smuggled it in. It
was too late for that to matter, but he did answer my
question. The bulge was indeed a handgun. I made no
response to his comment about the group. By then we
were in the main tunnel.

"Okay, you wait here until I distract the guard,"
Leon told me. He pointed to a dimly lighted side tunnel.
"I won't be long."

"Leon," I said, unable to wait any longer. "Exactly

what did you mean when you said it was being taken care of—the project, I mean? Are we in any danger?"

He hesitated at first, as though it were still his personal secret, but then he casually spoke the words that started icy fingers walking up and down my spine.

"No. We're not in any danger, but we can't stay around. There's another explosive in the lab, set for a couple of hours from now. And it's a *big* one."

chapter
EIGHTEEN

"You've got an explosive in the lab?" I echoed unbelievingly. I was closer to panic than ever before, but whatever else happened, I didn't want to give Leon any reason to do something violent. "Wasn't there any other way?" I asked cautiously.

"Oh, sure. I could have given them each individual appointments and shot them one by one when they came in."

"No," I said, ignoring the sarcasm. "I mean, did Krongard say that they all had to die?" If so, that sounded like an even harsher Krongard than the one I had met.

"Well, not actually." Leon came surprisingly close to looking embarrassed, but he extricated himself without much effort. "He said to stop the project and to get word out if I needed help. Well, it's damn near impossible to get word out now, because they tightened security. Anyway," he added as an apparent afterthought, "this way, Krongard will really owe me one."

The knot of fear in my stomach tightened. Things

were beginning to make sense. "Leon, you knew that the project was set up to *eliminate* scapescope, didn't you?"

"Sure, everyone did." Fortunately he must have had enough on his mind not to realize that I wasn't supposed to know. I hoped that he wouldn't think about it.

"Then why didn't Krongard know that?"

"If he knew that right off, he'd probably have melted this mountain down. Then where would we have been?"

"So you passed on the story about a long-range scapescope so that you could stay on, do the job, and collect your reward?"

"Exactly."

"Good thinking." I tried to say it in a serious tone and hoped that he would take it that way. "But how sure can you be that the explosive will take care of the whole job? Suppose some people leave the lab before the explosion?"

"I said it was big. We don't want to be anywhere in the complex when that thing goes off. And I'd better get moving. Just wait here. I'm going to send Merle back inside." Leon gave me what he probably thought was an encouraging grin. It wasn't.

An objection froze in my throat. I'd pushed him enough already. As his footsteps grew fainter I considered running back to the lab right then, but I didn't do it. Suppose he could detonate it from here? No, he said he didn't want to be inside when it went. My thoughts were pounding away when I heard Leon call me.

Rounding the corner, I realized why I hadn't heard Merle going back to the complex. He was lying facedown in the tunnel, his spindly arms splayed at unnatural angles. I knew then what must have happened, but a compulsion to eliminate any doubt drew me closer to him. Sure enough. There was a small charred spot at the base of his skull. Leon was a good shot or had been close to him.

I felt suddenly weak and nauseated. I had never seen anyone dead before, particularly not someone who had just been murdered.

"Come on," Leon called again. He sounded casual but slightly impatient.

I had to clear my throat before I could talk. "Why?" I asked as I slowly approached Leon. "I thought you were going to send him back."

"Don't be stupid. I'm not assigned here tonight. The minute he got back they'd know something was wrong."

"But you just killed him."

"What's the difference? They'll all be dead in an hour or two anyway. Come here, dammit. There are two buttons that have to be pressed simultaneously to get the door open. There's an override in the lab, but we can't very well ask them to activate it."

Multiple critical conclusions telescoped into that tiny instant in time just before I moved. First, Leon was crazy, at least by my standards. I'd never seen a personal power drive that strong, and he was obviously prepared to kill everyone in the complex. He undoubtedly even had some excuse that would explain why it was absolutely necessary and how he barely managed to get out in time. Krongard would lap it all up. Leon must have been blinded to the fact that I had a sister in the group, or assumed that I would be as willing as he was to sacrifice anyone who was in the way.

Second, even if I went with Leon, chances were that he would kill me shortly. He had lied to me only minutes before. He didn't need anyone to share the glory, or to let it slip that he had known the nature of the project for a long time.

Third, I didn't have any more chances coming after

this one. If I went out there and pushed that damned button, that would be my last act.

Fourth, none of the first three reasons mattered very much, since Lisa and Pat were in the lab with the bomb. I had to get back there.

"Okay. Okay. I'm coming," I said to Leon while I searched for alternatives. Overpowering him would be unlikely. Stalling would be just as hard. The only way was simply to run. But I needed time. "Just a second, Leon," I said, trying to put concern in my voice. "I thought I saw someone in there." I pointed to a side corridor that joined the main tunnel on the opposite side, several meters up from the tunnel we had taken to get here.

"You're sure?" Leon asked skeptically but softly.

"Pretty sure. I saw rapid movement—something white moved against that dark section on the left."

"Wait here a minute." He moved to investigate, the pistol in his hand.

I didn't know how long to wait. If he gave up before I started to run, I wouldn't gain anything. And if I started too soon, he'd hear me immediately.

In my eagerness to flee I must have started too soon. Leon had just turned a corner, shielding him from view, when I slowly stepped back to the mouth of the tunnel. Another moment's hesitation and then I turned and ran.

I tried to sacrifice speed to keep down the noise of my running, but my heart was pounding so loudly I couldn't judge the noise level that my strides generated. Either I had been too noisy or too slow.

The beam caught me on the top of my left shoulder, pain lancing through my arm and chest. I stumbled but kept on going. A desperate backward glance told me that I now had just enough curve of the tunnel between us to keep him from trying again until he gained still more or we reached a straightaway.

The waves of pain oscillated between tolerable and excruciating, but the wound must have been just on the surface or near it. The pain pulsed along my shoulder every time a new step jolted my body. Fortunately the burn must have self-cauterized, because there was no stream of blood. That's a help, I thought crazily. At least there wouldn't be a trail of blood crumbs to lead Hansel and Gretel to me.

An instant later stairs and a door loomed ahead. I took the steps at least three at a time and almost lost my footing at the top. Two sparkling points of light against the wall ahead told me without looking back that Leon still had a hefty charge in his gun and that he hadn't got bored with the chase. I could only assume he wasn't using it on automatic in an effort to keep me alive— temporarily.

I turned the corner, putting myself out of range, and hesitated only a sliver of a second. If only I could take the corridor directly in front of me—but to do so now would be suicidal. The hall was long and straight and narrow. Leon could just lean back and shoot until he finished his job.

I took the stairs instead two at a time, keeping well away from the railing. Shortly after I left the stairs another set of pounding footsteps started up them. So that was all the lead I had.

I raced down the corridor to my right, frantically trying to orient myself so I could find a way to get to a branch in the corridors far enough ahead of Leon so that he would have to guess which way I had gone. Even a fifty percent chance would be better than what I had now. Or maybe I could hide in a room long enough for him to pass by. No. I ruled that out except as a last resort. With his gun it wouldn't be much of a contest if I guessed wrong.

With two more turns behind me, I slowed so I could

hear Leon's footsteps. Then I stopped entirely. Nothing. Leon must have listened to me and decided to slow his pace. Or for all I knew, he could be taking another route that would put him ahead of me, directly in my path.

The chill I had felt when Leon told me about the explosives was back, mingling with the throbbing in my shoulder. I somehow felt even more threatened now than I had when he was pounding after me. I started walking as fast and as noiselessly as I could. He couldn't have moved fast enough to get ahead of me, so I'd be outsmarting myself if I doubled back at this point.

At the next intersection, a cross, I peered in both sideways directions and then went straight, hoping to put as much distance as possible between us. As I peeked around the corner at the following intersection I thought about how vulnerable I would be if Leon should happen to be in that corridor.

What I really needed was a flexible fiber-optic viewer or a small periscope. Even a mirror.

But there *were* mirrors around—the circular, convex ones that were mounted in some of the intersections to prevent collisions. Two junctions later I found one. I had to jump to reach it, but my weight was enough to rip the single mounting connection from the back of the mirror.

The noise worried me. Tearing the mirror loose had been quieter than I expected, but it still seemed loud enough to summon Leon. I quickened my pace to put distance between me and the broken mirror-support. Three flat mirrors could form a corner reflector that would let me bounce Leon's beam back at him, but I didn't have them and I didn't trust Leon to aim for them.

Three corridors later I was eternally grateful for the

mirror. I was at one side of a T intersection, ready to cross it. Before I did, I edged closer to the turn and pushed about a centimeter of the mirror past the beam that framed the corner.

I was glad I hadn't exposed my head to look. Leon was almost halfway along the corridor.

I clenched the mirror more tightly and retreated, almost running, while trying to be quiet. If it hadn't been for the *whoosh* of the air circulation system, he probably could have heard me.

Maybe he *had* heard me. I reached the next intersection just in time to look with my mirror and see Leon reach the corner I had just left and turn in my direction. I watched, paralyzed, as he put his head near the wall for a moment and then continued. He went to the other wall then, maybe trying to see as much parallax as possible. I pulled back my mirror, worried that he might have sharp enough eyes to detect it. Maybe he could. Maybe he had augmented eyes.

I had to get away. I ran lightly to the next corner. Perhaps I should have kept on running, but I was compelled to know where Leon was. I repeated the procedure with the mirror and watched in horror as Leon picked the right direction once again. What were the odds against that?

I fled. At the back of my mind there was a faint voice pleading with me not to make so much noise, but I barely listened. Leon had looked so *calm*. I had to get out of the area. I had to get back to the lab.

But I had to lose Leon first. If he got back there with me, he'd probably resort to killing people individually rather than wait for the explosion.

I reached another stairwell, but instead of going back to the first floor as Leon might expect, I scrambled up to the third floor. This time I ran the length of the longest corridor. A pain in my side from running joined the throbbing in my shoulder.

The mirror vibrated in my hands. There were small vibrations as my hands shook from the tension, and large sways as I gasped lungfuls of air. I still wasn't in good shape for that altitude.

There was no sign of Leon yet. My mind had time to slow down and let me observe my surroundings. I was back in the area near the local-node computer room. The corridor I had rushed through was reasonably well lighted, but behind me the hall grew dimmer.

I had begun to relax still more when a small flicker of motion in the mirror caught my attention. Leon was coming down the corridor toward me. Damn him. How did he know?

And then I realized. The explosive he had me put in the local-node computer room had been fitted with a transponder so it could be located easily. Now I must be wearing it or its cousin. But it could be anywhere—in my hair, stuck on the back of my shirt or pants. What's more, there was no time left to search.

I turned to run, and before I traveled ten meters I had an inspiration. I hadn't been there, but on this floor the map had shown a long corridor that bottlenecked at one door. If I could get there enough ahead of Leon to lock or jam the door, I could probably gain enough time to get to the lab to warn them before it was too late. Surely they must have some weapons, too, and I could give them enough advance notice.

I didn't stop to peer around any corners. I just ran as fast as I could. The corridors grew darker as I approached the hallway I needed. This route took me back into the seldom-used area. Fearing that Leon would hear my footsteps, but not daring to slow down, I finally realized what he had been doing when he put his head next to the walls. This was a mostly metal building. He could probably feel the vibrations caused by my movement.

I ran down the final corridor in almost pitch-dark. A faint glimmer off the wall at the end kept me from running into anything, but I narrowly missed another fire extinguisher.

I reached the end of the corridor and turned right to see the doorway that I had to jam. It was right where I had expected it to be.

But there was a big problem.

I was too late. It was *already* locked—from the other side. In an almost overpowering rage, I kicked at the lock to break it off.

All I did was hurt my foot.

I had outsmarted myself. Not only had I lost my chance to delay Leon for any length of time, but there I was in a dead end, helplessly waiting for Leon to find me.

He might be crazy, but he didn't strike me as absent-minded.

chapter
NINETEEN

I stood panting in front of the locked door, my body stiff with frustration and anger. There was no doubt that Leon must be calmly approaching along the corridor that was my only way out.

The next moment showed that assumption to be all too painfully accurate. Leon called out from what sounded like a long way down the hall.

"I'll bet you didn't know that door was sealed. It's just you and me, Cavantalo." Echoes bouncing off the walls boosted the gravelly quality in his voice. "If you come out in fifteen seconds and push that button for me, I'll kill you quickly." He paused for a moment, making me wonder if he were coming ahead anyway. "If you make it hard for me, and I have to use explosives to get out, you'll last longer than you'd like, believe me."

Leon couldn't have known how much I liked having options, but even though he had given me two, I wasn't particularly pleased about either selection. Actually there was only one choice; I had to fight.

To do that, I needed a weapon and a hell of a surprise. Leon's gun was an overpowering advantage. I swung back to see if any of the doorways that I had passed led to anything usable.

As I paused in the nearest opening, trying to see into the almost total darkness, I glimpsed something familiar out of the corner of my eye.

Hanging there on the wall was one of those ever-present hazards: a fire extinguisher. I wrenched it from its holder and examined it in the dim light. I had visions of spraying Leon in the face as he was about to squeeze the trigger, but beneath the grime on the label was an expiration date for over fifty years ago.

I didn't know much about fire extinguishers, but I could imagine that whatever was inside had long since coagulated into an unmovable mass. On the other hand, maybe it would still spew foam, but it would simply no longer be effective against fire. Could I take the chance?

And there was still the bug. Leon must know exactly where I was. I had to get rid of it. But where was it?

It had to be in my hair or stuck to my clothes. I frantically ran a comb through my hair. The transponder Leon had had in the package was much larger than standard government tracers. It would probably have shown up if it was there.

Nothing. So it was on my clothes—probably. As fast as I could, I stripped off my T-shirt and shorts. My shoulder quivered uncontrollably as my skin flexed and the material scraped across the burn. I kicked my sneakers into the darkened room and threw the rest of my clothes after them.

I stood there shivering in my underwear, feeling scared and foolish at the same time. A faint movement of air evaporated some of my cold sweat, chilling me more. My clothes, and therefore the bug, lay in the cor-

ner of the office across the hall, and I stood with the fire
extinguisher just inside the doorway opposite. In spite
of having a plan, I was not confident.

There was way too much margin for error. Leon was
strong and quick. The fire extinguisher might not work.
I might not be fast enough. Even after I sprayed Leon,
he might still have the presence of mind to sweep the
area around him with a pulsed beam.

Then I knew what I had to do. Two mental barriers
came down and I could see an alternative that would increase my chances.

My wristcomp was useless for communicating with
the group, since the local-node computer was disabled,
but it still had all of its normal off-line functions.

Including audio record and playback.

I put it into record mode and uttered a phrase with
what I hoped sounded like a terrified voice. That didn't
take too much acting ability. As soon as I had turned
playback on for sound activation, I put the wristcomp
with the stack of clothes and pushed them behind a dirty
military desk.

An old pen from the desk served to test the setup. The
sound it made being tossed lightly against the wall was
loud enough to trigger the playback. I pulled the office
door almost closed and then scurried back across the
hall.

Just in time. Less than thirty seconds later a faint
outline in my mirror told me that Leon had just turned
the final corner in the hallway and was cautiously approaching. Maybe the darkness made him nervous.

I held the fire extinguisher ready, the metal cold
against my skin. I tried to breathe quietly despite my
racing heartbeat. If this didn't work, I would have
failed Lisa. And the prospect of a slow, painful death
while knowing I had certified death for the others was

something I tried to force out of my thoughts.

The sounds from the corridor were nearly imperceptible. I almost felt rather than heard Leon's approach. The *whoosh* of the air circulation system covered most of what little sound he made, but fortunately it helped me too.

Leon couldn't have been checking out each office as he went. He was coming too fast. Good. The sounds slowed down as he approached the office containing my clothes, which confirmed my conviction that he was using a direction finder. There was a faint noise that sounded like he was putting something in his pocket.

As he neared, I felt a strong urge to stop breathing, but the rational part of my brain told me that he couldn't hear *that* well.

The sounds stopped in front of the doorway to my hiding place. I didn't dare look because Leon's peripheral vision might catch me even in the poor lighting. He waited there in the hall a moment longer, and then things started to happen incredibly fast.

The next sound had to be Leon kicking open the door across the hall. The fact that he was very close to me was verified by the next noise, a faint *pinging* sound, repeated several times. It was the soft fire-control indicator on his gun *pinging* each time a new pulse was fired. Leon was taking no chances; he was sweeping the room that should have contained me.

One last noise reached me before I moved. I heard my voice come from the other room, from my wristcomp, and it said, "Oh, God, Leon—no. . . ."

In that instant, when his attention had to be focused on the source of that sound, I moved.

I don't know whether he heard me or he just had unbelievably well-developed instincts, but as I came at him from behind, Leon started to turn. I held the fire extinguisher over my head now, realizing that the only reliable use I could put it to was that of a blunt instrument.

He moved almost out of the path of the downward swing of the fire extinguisher, but my thrust was strong, reinforced by frustration, fear, and the knowledge that this was the only chance for Lisa and Pat.

The blow knocked Leon off balance, but terrifyingly fast he started recovering and swinging that deadly gun around toward me. The inertia of the fire extinguisher made it hard to hit him again rapidly, but still strengthened by motivations that weren't all obvious to me, I pulled it back and swung again.

This time it worked. Leon, perhaps partly dazed, couldn't move quickly enough to get far enough out of the way. The fire extinguisher connected violently just over his left ear, and he dropped limply to the floor.

Elated but cautious, I grabbed the gun. Once I was satisfied that he truly was unconscious, I rapidly searched him. The examination yielded two more packages of explosives and two small, unidentifiable electronic devices fastened in a belt that he wore inside his shirt.

I put the explosives in the hall and dragged Leon into the room that he had scorched in numerous places. I kicked my clothes into the hall and, from the outside, used the gun on the lock until the doorknob wouldn't turn.

I stood there motionless for more than a minute, trying to let my breathing and my heart relax. My legs were wobbly as I pulled on my clothes and put on my shoes. I didn't want to bother with the T-shirt because of my shoulder, but I was cold. Partially recovered, I stuck the gun in my waistband and began to run. The run quickly became a jog. My body felt drained of energy.

After I almost fell down the stairs, I slowed down still more, but only to a moderate jog. A couple of minutes later, after what seemed like ten or fifteen minutes, I reached the lab.

I punched in the combination and did so a second time as the lock refused to open. Damn. Maybe I could have gone back for the explosives to blow the door in, but I wasn't sure how much energy I had left—or how much time.

The door reverberated with my slow, thudding kicks. Surely someone must come to investigate.

Someone did. In a minute the lock clicked and an elderly, mustached man whom I faintly recognized opened the door.

"What the hell's going—oh, it's you." If he noticed that I looked peaked, he kept it to himself.

"I have to come in—" I began.

"Not a chance." He started to close the door.

"Wait a minute. There's a bomb in there, set to go off soon. I'm coming in." I moved to do so.

"Nice try. So I'm supposed to say, 'Oh, gosh, come right in'? Go away."

As he started to push the door shut again, I gave up trying to be a nice guy. I pulled the gun out of my belt and pointed it at him. "You see this?" I didn't wait for his reply. "Back off. What I said is true. If I have to injure one person to keep the rest of you alive, that's just bad luck. Yours."

I pushed the door open. The old man offered no resistance this time, and a short walk took us to the main lab area. The reception was unenthusiastic. I was sick to death of being unpopular.

As soon as we were noticed, the inhabitants turned into a disorganized throng. Seeing me there with a pistol must have brought some very unpleasant images to their minds. In a moment, once everyone knew I was there, the room quieted down.

"There's a bomb in here," I announced into the uneasy silence. "And it's set—" That was as far as I got before the clamor started up again. A moment later I continued. "It's set to go off pretty soon." I looked at my wrist, but my wristcomp was still back in the room with Leon. "What time is it now?"

No one answered me. I looked around at their angry faces and noticed two people coming toward me from different parts of the room: Lisa and Don.

"I didn't set the bomb, dammit. Lisa, would you tell them?" I asked. "I'm trying to help, but there's not much time." I sat down wearily on a nearby desk.

Lisa looked around the room briefly, probably seeing what I did: a mixture of surprise and hostility.

"He's telling us the truth," she said rapidly. "I don't know why it's here or who put it here, but if Mike says there's a bomb here, you can depend on it." She went on to give a greatly abbreviated summary of what I had found out.

"What does it look like?" Don asked when Lisa finished.

I gave them a description of the original package I had put in the local-node computer room. They found one like it twenty minutes later. It was a hell of a lot bigger than the other one, though. No others turned up in continued searching.

They could have sent some of the best brains of the group to another part of the complex during the search, but Don never suggested it and neither did anyone else. Maybe it made the difference, having a few more people tearing the place apart. I don't know. We couldn't tell how much time was left by looking at the timer.

It had been concealed against one of the structural supports, above the hanging ceiling tiles. It wasn't a great hiding place, but then Leon hadn't anticipated an intense search.

Lisa came over and put her hand on my good shoulder. "It was a shock to see you leading Jules in here with that pistol." Jules must have been the doorman. I smiled weakly, thinking about it.

Pat and Don joined us. I told them the rest of the story and where to find Leon. Don took it all in impassively, but occasional pain flickered through Pat's eyes.

"Don't worry about not trusting me," I told Pat when I finished the story. "It looked pretty bad. I probably would have done the same." Lisa smiled ruefully.

I hoped that Pat felt a little less guilty than before. "I guess I don't know you as well as I used to," she said. "Let's have a nice, long talk when this is over."

"I'd like that."

Don spoke up again. "How about finishing all this work?" To me he said, "We're about an hour away if everything checks out okay." He gave me more of a smile than he ever had before.

The others had been cleaning up after the search. I asked if there was anything I could do and was told to relax and wait. A dark-haired woman I didn't know took time to patch my shoulder and give me a painkiller.

Sometime later they had to wake me. I had been so tired that the constant murmur of activity in the lab had eventually faded into the background.

Lisa, Pat, and Don were hovering over me.

"When do you cut the ribbon and throw the switch?" I asked.

Don answered. "We already did. There wasn't any ceremony."

"And you won't know for a while if it works?"

"That's right. We have to sit and wait for several days to be sure."

chapter
TWENTY

As we waited on test results during the next few days, I spent most of my time with Lisa. She wasn't participating in the post-disturbance testing, so her work was completed.

Lisa and I were talking in the cafeteria when the meeting was announced. The others must have completed the preliminary testing. The cafeteria itself was one of the most convenient rooms for a large gathering, so we just sat as the group filed in.

"Your efforts have been successful," Don started out, coming straight to the point. "Visibility is decreasing, just as predicted. Probably within the next two weeks the government is going to realize that this is not just another normal field disturbance. Scapescope will soon be entirely useless."

I had almost stopped paying attention, but Don changed all that with his next few words.

"However," he continued, "we have created a potential problem." There was a ripple of noise from the people who hadn't participated in the final testing.

"Let me go back to the pond analogy for a moment. What we wanted to do was stir up some mud in the pond, and hold it in suspension for a long time. We did that. What we've also done, though, is to set up waves on the surface of the pond. We're not sure yet, but the time wave peaks look to be one or two centuries apart.

"The most surprising part is that we are able to receive crude images from those peaks, as though we were looking through the air across the surface of the pond. It will take us a while to determine how to eliminate the view, and to satisfy our curiosity.

"We may be busy longer than we thought. There's still a lot to do. But we'll probably have a lot more leverage with the government, now that the short-term problem has changed to a long-range question. And we do have a virtual monopoly on leading-edge scapescope technology."

There was a flurry of questions, but Don had already explained the only part that I could easily follow.

"I guess that's bad news and good news," Lisa said. "Your job won't be the same, but eventually you can probably go back to working with the same people, if you want."

I waited a moment, thinking about Arthur, before I asked, "What's the *good* news?"

I glanced at Lisa and grinned. The smile that she returned could have transformed a recluse into a social butterfly. I certainly couldn't see any problem with staying around for quite a while. Some of the newness seemed to be wearing off, but below it was a growing layer of contentment.

It felt good, too, to see the changes in Lisa. Overhearing a few comments to her like, "You sure seem happy.

What's happening?'' was infinitely better than hearing, "You look different. Are you putting on a little weight?''

No. There wouldn't be any problem with staying around for quite a while. I wanted to see Seldon again, and thank him, but there would be time.

I looked at Lisa. Maybe you can never go back, but, if you're exceptionally lucky, you can take it with you.